KID O'FALLON LAY IN THE DUST, SOBBING PATHETICALLY.

"Don't kill me," he pleaded. "I ain't done nothing. Not really."

"How many men you killed?" asked Slocum. He cocked his Colt. "How many boys? Did you even stop there? What about women?"

"Never killed a woman."

Slocum's finger twitched on the trigger. The way O'Fallon said that combined fear and longing. He hadn't killed any women because of lack of opportunity rather than scruples.

"Don't shoot me," O'Fallon begged.

"I wouldn't waste my ammunition," said Slocum. The leer on O'Fallon's face quickly changed to terror when he saw what Slocum intended.

OTHER BOOKS BY JAKE LOGAN

JAKE LOGAN

SLOCUM AND
THE CLAIM JUMPERS

BERKLEY BOOKS, NEW YORK

SLOCUM AND THE CLAIM JUMPERS

A Berkley Book/published by arrangement with
the author

PRINTING HISTORY
Berkley edition/September 1987

ISBN: 0-425-10188-6

A BERKLEY BOOK ® TM 757,375
Berkley Books are published by The Berkley Publishing Group,
200 Madison Avenue, New York, N.Y. 10016.
The name "BERKLEY" and the "B" logo
are trademarks belonging to Berkley Publishing Corporation.

PRINTED IN THE UNITED STATES OF AMERICA

10 9 8 7 6 5 4 3 2 1

1

John Slocum laid the cards face down on the table in front of him. The others around the table joked and drank heavily. Not Slocum. He needed a stake before leaving Colorado Springs, and Lady Luck had turned her back on him. A week earlier, Denver had shown him no hospitality. He had left that thriving town only minutes before the marshal started thinking about posses and lynchings.

None of that had been his fault. Slocum had been unlucky enough to be in the same place as Kid O'Fallon when the young backshooter had brutally gunned down two patrons of the Brown Palace.

Slocum had done his share of killing, but of these murders he was innocent.

"Bad luck," he snorted.

"Whass that?" slurred the cowboy across the table. The man's hands moved in jerky motions, showing he was on the verge of passing out from the cheap whiskey he had been swilling all night. Slocum did not care about the man's condition—after this hand Slocum would have his stake and could move on.

The five cards face down on the table in front of him would win enough for him to leave Colorado Springs and vanish to the West.

1

"You got all your money in the pot?" the cowboy asked.

Something in the way the man spoke alerted Slocum. The cowboy wasn't half as drunk as he had seemed just a few seconds ago. Slocum's quick green eyes searched the faces of the others at the table. Two sat impassively, nothing to be read in their expressions. The third smirked. The corners of his mouth turned up just enough in a mocking grin to tell Slocum that he had been had.

He was so eager to get a stake that he had neglected to watch the game for a spell before dealing himself in. At least two of these men worked together to fleece unsuspecting players. Slocum could not be sure that all four weren't involved.

Slocum rocked back in his chair, balancing on the back two legs. This let him move easier if he had to get to the Colt slung in his cross-draw holster. This simple move on his part brought others from the bar like buzzards waiting for their prey to die.

He saw two men with shotguns at either end of the long teak bar. The barkeep stood back, nervously looking from side to side, the tips of his handlebar mustache twitching. In the mirror behind the bar Slocum saw the reflection of a man on the stairs leading to the second-floor cribs. In that man's hands rested a Winchester.

If Slocum made any move these men did not like, he'd find a pound of hot lead in his belly and back.

"Don't reckon a full house, kings over fives, wins, does it?" he asked, trying to keep the tension he felt from his words.

"Mister, that's the best damn hand I seen you with all night. Better'n anything I had tonight, too," the not-so-drunk cowboy said.

Slocum waited. The rest had to come. It did.

"But it ain't gonna beat four treys. Never cottoned to them little cards, unless I have enough of them." The cowboy raked in their pot—and all Slocum's money.

"Hold on," Slocum said. He heard hammers cocking

and the Winchester dropping down on the top rail to steady its aim on his back. "You forgot something."

"What might that be, mister?" the cowboy asked. Slocum saw the way he checked to be sure his friends were all covering him before speaking.

"Since you got all my money, the least you can do is buy me a drink."

Slocum's green eyes locked with the man's muddy brown ones. The cowboy's face wrinkled up into a broad smile.

"Reckon he's got a point. Jesse, bring the man a bottle. None of that trade whiskey. A good bottle."

Slocum accepted the bottle as the best he was likely to get in Colorado Springs. It wasn't trade whiskey laced with black powder and enough nails to give it body, but it wasn't much better. But by the time Slocum had drained it, he was in no condition to care.

He wobbled slightly as he left the saloon. No one paid him any attention. He had shown himself to be a good loser, even knowing he had been cheated. Slocum stood in the doorway and looked back. The cowboy and his friends worked their card sharp ways on a new sucker. Slocum shook his head. His luck over the past few months had been bad, but he hadn't thought it could get worse.

The cold night air cut through the whiskey fog that had descended on his senses. Slocum sucked in a lungful of the pine and juniper scented air and knew that he might be broke, but things could be worse.

He could have ended up dead in the alley behind the saloon if he had raised a ruckus. Slocum did not often make a mistake like he'd just done, but he was philosophical about it.

"Should never rush things," he said to no one in particular. He spun, hand on his Colt, when he got an answer.

"Good advice. Reckon you didn't take it yourself?" A lucifer flared in the night, illuminating a grizzled old man sitting in a chair on the plank sidewalk.

"Course not," Slocum said. "Good advice is always ignored, even when you're giving it to yourself."

"Come set a spell," the man invited. "Don't get too many along this time of night who aren't drunk on their asses."

Slocum took the rickety, straight-backed chair next to the man. Slocum fumbled inside his jacket and pulled out a quirly. The old man silently lit another lucifer and held it until Slocum puffed dark blue clouds of smoke.

"Bad whiskey, bad smoke, but the town looks nice. Quiet, except for the saloon," observed Slocum. He puffed slowly, savoring the way the smoke went deep and warm into his lungs and convinced him that life was, indeed, worthwhile.

"Can't expect anything but bad whiskey at Crazy Harry's. Don't drink there, myself." The old man spat. "Truth to tell, I don't drink much of anywhere these days. Burns like fire in my gut. Doc Sampson said it'd kill me if I kept on. So I stopped." The old man chuckled. "Outlived Doc. Outlived the young squirt who took over his practice, too."

"Is Colorado Springs always this quiet?"

"Hell, it's been this way for well nigh six months. Ever since that damnfool gold strike."

"Over Cripple Creek way?" asked Slocum. He puffed slowly.

"Biggest strike since Sutter out on the American River in Forty-eight, or so they say. Damn good way of going broke."

"I'm already broke," Slocum said.

The man chuckled. "Then there's not much keeping you from going over to Cripple Creek to find your fortune, though you don't have the look of a miner about you."

Slocum didn't need to be told that. The worn handle of his Colt, the way he moved, the way people fell silent when he came into a room—all branded him as something more than a miner. But he had gone tin-panning, had run a placer mine for a spell up in the

Sierra Madres, had even worked a while as a hard-rock miner. Not a single stint had got him the fabulous wealth he had sought.

Slocum shook his head slowly. He wasn't sure if this wasn't for the best. What would he do with the kind of wealth so many sought and so few found? Gamble? Drift from place to place? He did those already. Slocum had no intention of settling down. What good was a pile of money to a man like him?

"Wish I had a couple coins to rub together in my pocket," he said, more to himself than to the old man beside him.

"You lost everything at Crazy Harry's," the man said. It was not a question. "Damnfool thing to do, getting into a poker game there. They work together real good. Not a single greenhorn gets through without losing a wad." The old man spat, coughed, and puffed hard on his cigar, his head vanishing totally in a cloud of smoke.

"They fleece everyone?"

"That's not hard to do, not these days. Gamblers steer clear of Crazy Harry's. And the miners? Hell, when they're in town you can't keep them out of the place. They flock in, all het up and ready to make millions in the gold field. They're ripe for the pickin'. They're already gambling everything on one fever dream. Crazy Harry just relieves them of the burden of their poke."

"But not the dream," said Slocum. He had seen the fire burning in men's eyes when they spoke of hitting the mother lode in a new gold strike. It was worse than gambling fever; it was worse than robbing the poor devils of a few dollars.

That fire never burned itself out—not until the man trying to grab hold of it died.

"You seem too sensible to lose. What's your problem?"

"No problem," Slocum lied. "Just over-eager. Doesn't happen much, but it does happen."

"Where you headin'? To Cripple Creek?"

"Might be, but not to mine. Are there jobs there? I'm not opposed to doing a day's work for a day's pay."

"The Independence Mine over Battle Mountain way is having trouble getting men. That the kind of work you hankerin' for?"

Slocum thought on it. The backbreaking hours of a hard-rock miner buried far underground for eight hours at a spell didn't appeal to him. He had done it and didn't much like it.

"Anything else?"

"There's always something else, if you know the angles. They got men up there who are getting rich in gold and never so much as set foot on a claim."

"Some things never change. Reckon I can make enough in a month's time to keep going west."

"What's to the west? Never mind," the old man said quickly. "Ain't none of my business. And what you have in mind to look for in Cripple Creek ain't my business neither."

"How long is it to Cripple Creek on horseback?"

"Depends on your horse. Strong, good horse able to take the steep climb, not more'n a day. Otherwise, you might as well shoot the horse rather than try. You might consider the stage. Leaves here at dawn every day. Nickel a mile going in, dime a mile return."

"Why's that?"

"Sorta encourages 'em to make a good claim. Stage owner figures they can afford it, one way or the other. Either they's broker'n shit and are desperate to leave, in which case they'll scare up the fare somehow, or they hit it big."

"In which case, they can afford it."

"And brag on it," the old man finished.

Slocum fell silent. He would have to ride. Even at the lower rate going to the boom town, he had no money to spare. He sat and talked idly with the old man until he heard the sound of horse's hooves. Slocum turned and tried to determine the source.

Even the old man looked up, surprised. "No one's on the road this time of night. Not unless..." His voice trailed off. He didn't have to finish for Slocum to know what he meant.

Only road agents would be out and about at this hour. Most of Colorado Springs slept. Even the boisterous crowd at Crazy Harry's had quieted, the largest part of them drifting away to wife or lover or solitary bed.

"It might be your sheriff," said Slocum.

"Not likely. Last I heard, he was out serving process, way the hell and gone over at Karval. His worthless deputy's up in the hills with an Injun squaw. Reckon it's time for me to turn in."

The old man heaved himself to his feet. He looked down at Slocum. "Better find yourself cover. If'n it's outlaws, they get mean when they start shootin' up the place."

"Good night," said Slocum. He watched the old man shuffle off, turn down an alley, and vanish from sight. Slocum stood, settled his Colt into place, and headed for the stables. He had intended to sleep with his horse, anyway. Checking the animal seemed a smart thing to do if there were road agents drifting around the town.

A lathered black stallion stood outside the stables, snorting and pawing at the ground. Slocum saw no trace of the huge animal's rider. He skirted the stallion, not wanting to tangle with those heavy hooves, and slipped inside the stable.

The horses inside stirred nervously, whinnying. One mare tried to kick down her stall. Something—just the stallion outside?—spooked the horses.

Slocum slipped his Colt from its holster and moved softer than any ghost through the stables. He stopped at the stall of his grey gelding. Someone had rifled through his gear. Without checking carefully, he couldn't tell if anything had been stolen.

He looked for the stableboy who slept in the tack room. Slocum found him. The boy's head lolled to one side at an impossible angle. Someone had cut his throat and damned near twisted his head off afterwards.

Every nerve in Slocum's body came alive. He heard the faintest of noises. Odors took on a different meaning. He saw through shadows. And his hand firmly gripped his Colt. He was ready to kill the son of a bitch who had butchered a young boy.

A scent different from what he would expect in a stable rose to his nostrils. He sniffed harder—and knew who the killer was.

Kid O'Fallon doused himself with rose water until he reeked. Few men said anything about it. O'Fallon had killed more than his share for less than remarking on the way he smelled. Slocum knew he had to watch his back carefully. O'Fallon hadn't killed all those men in fair fights. The rumors were that each had been backshot.

Remembering what he had done in Denver ought to have been warning enough. Seeing the dead stableboy made Slocum believe the rumors.

He edged along the back wall of the stable, then slipped outside into the cool mountain air. The light breeze blowing down from the Rockies turned the sweat on his body to ice. Slocum circled the stable, hunting for any sign of O'Fallon. He found nothing.

The shriek of pain coming from inside the stable chilled him all the way to his belly. It was almost human, but Slocum recognized it as a horse in agony. He held back and did not burst into the stables; O'Fallon would be waiting to bushwhack him.

"What's the matter, Slocum?" came the high, squeaky voice of Kid O'Fallon. "I know you're out there. Or have you hightailed it out of town? You run off again, like you did in Denver?"

Slocum found a small window in the side with the tack room. He levered it up, wincing at the squeaks of protest as dried wood slid on the equally dry frame. Slocum slid through the window head first, his Colt pointed at the door leading into the stall area. He carefully avoided stepping on the dead stableboy and peered into the darkened stalls.

He saw the severed head of his horse in the middle of the stable. What O'Fallon had done with the body, Slocum couldn't guess. Probably still in the stall. The horse had been too heavy for the small killer to drag around easily.

"You got a hankerin' to kill me, Slocum? You were supposed to keep the marshal busy in Denver while I waltzed away. But they're looking for me. I got a posse hot on my trail, and they don't even want to see your ugly face no more."

Slocum ducked down and moved into the stable. If O'Fallon was waiting for him, the killer would be watching the main doors.

A small, dark form moved across the stable. Slocum's Colt rose and a heavy .45 slug cut through the air.

"Bloody hell!" swore O'Fallon. "How'd you get behind me, Slocum? You see what I did to your horse? I'm gonna do that to you! You were supposed to take the heat in Denver."

"Sorry your frame didn't work, O'Fallon," said Slocum. He moved quickly. He didn't think he had hit the killer. This fight couldn't last long. If it seemed to be going against the kid, O'Fallon would turn tail and run like a scared rabbit.

Slocum wanted him dead.

Slocum climbed up onto a stall divider and worked his way up to the hayloft. From this vantage point he had a good view of the floor. During the War he had been a sniper for the Confederacy—one of the best. Many's the day he had sat on a hilltop and waited for the glint of sunlight off a Union officer's gold braid. A slow, careful sighting, a trigger squeeze, the heavy recoil, and the enemy troops found themselves without a leader.

In combat that kind of fighting took patience, skill, and rock-steady nerves. This was no different.

Slocum lay belly down in the loft and cocked his weapon. Only the horses stirred below. For the moment. Kid O'Fallon would get antsy, think maybe Slocum had left, think that maybe *he* should leave. When that happened, Slocum would be ready for the quick, killing shot.

"You cut your own throat, Slocum?" came the whining voice from below. "You'd do that, wouldn't you, just to rob me of the pleasure. Where the hell are you?"

Slocum shifted slightly in the direction of the voice. He made out two possible targets. He waited. No sense picking one and finding out he was wrong. He didn't want O'Fallon getting a chance to escape.

"Slocum?" The shrill voice overflowed with fear. O'Fallon was as much of a coward as Slocum had thought. "Where are you, you son of a bitch?"

Slocum homed in on the voice, then squeezed off a shot. The report echoed through the stable and started the horses kicking frantically at their stalls. The yelp of pain from O'Fallon, though, was Slocum's reward. He doubted he had seriously injured the bushwhacker, but he had slowed him down.

The squeak of the big doors opening brought Slocum up from his prone position. Slocum leaned out enough to get off another shot at Kid O'Fallon as he tried to escape. The bullet missed, but splinters flew into the killer's face.

Slocum jerked around and raced for the hayloft doors. He had no chance for a shot at O'Fallon once the kid got to his stallion. Slocum vaulted over bales of hay and skidded to a halt. He paused for a moment, took a deep breath, then kicked open the loft doors.

Four quick shots whistled past and crashed into the roof. "Take that, you son of a bitch!" shrieked O'Fallon from below. The kid had tried once more to ambush him.

And again, he had failed.

John Slocum fell forward onto his belly again, his Colt ready. O'Fallon had not mounted his horse. Slocum used a bullet to send the skittish horse jerking to the end of its tether. The bucking and pawing prevented Kid

O'Fallon from mounting—and left him an easy target in the stable yard.

"You won't get me. None of them ever will! You won't, you won't!"

O'Fallon's shrill voice cracked. Slocum hesitated. How old was O'Fallon? Sixteen? Perhaps seventeen?

A vision of the dead stableboy, who had been only twelve, flashed in front of Slocum. The way O'Fallon had decapitated the grey. The deaths in Denver. Everything about O'Fallon spoke of a crazed killer. His age did not matter.

Slocum squeezed the trigger and knocked O'Fallon's left leg out from under him. The kid tumbled forward, face down in the dust. Slocum swung out the block and tackle used to load bales of hay into the loft and used this to lower himself.

Kid O'Fallon lay in the dust, sobbing pathetically.

"Don't kill me," he pleaded. "I ain't done nothing. Not really."

"How many men you killed?" asked Slocum. He cocked his Colt. "How many boys? Did you ever stop there? What about women?"

"Never killed a woman."

Slocum's finger twitched on the trigger. The way O'Fallon said that combined fear and longing. He hadn't killed any women because of lack of opportunity rather than scruples.

"Don't shoot me," O'Fallon begged.

"I wouldn't waste my ammunition," said Slocum. The leer on O'Fallon's face quickly changed to terror when he saw what Slocum intended.

John Slocum leaned against a rail, hat pulled low to protect his eyes against the rising sun. The Concord stage bound for Cripple Creek would be along shortly, and Slocum held a ticket on it.

"You not ridin' up to the gold country?" asked a familiar voice. Slocum turned to see the old man he had spoken to the night before leaning back in his chair. He had discarded his smoke for a piece of wood partially whittled into a whistle. The old man smiled and held it up for Slocum to see. "For my grandson. Noisy little devil. Drives his ma crazy."

Slocum turned back. A cloud of dust rose out on the road. That had to be the stage.

"Strange things happening," the old man went on. "Take last night."

"What about last night?" asked Slocum, trying not to look interested.

"Seems we had something of an accident. Kid O'Fallon, some say."

Slocum held his tongue. There was nothing to say.

"Yes, right strange," the old man went on. "They found him this morning with his hands tied behind his back and a rope around his neck. Over at the stables. Looked as if someone had lynched him."

"Outlaws like him end up dangling from a rope all the time. So?"

"Right strange, as I was sayin'. Had a bullet in his thigh. Rope wasn't knotted for a hangman's noose, either. O'Fallon choked to death. Musta hung there for some time before he died."

Slocum looked around. Other passengers had gathered to take the stage to Cripple Creek: two men, both looking the part of gold miners; another man who might be a patent medicine salesman; and a pretty woman with a young girl.

"Figured O'Fallon was hoisted up on his horse, a feisty stallion. Kid probably tried to keep the horse still for a while."

"Maybe as long as five minutes," said Slocum.

The old man cocked his head to one side, then nodded knowingly. "No loss. Not when you consider Billy Alexander inside the stable with his throat slit, and a good-looking grey with his head plumb cut off. Figure O'Fallon might have done that, especially since a bloody knife was found stuck in his belt."

"He might have got the knife out and used it to free himself," said Slocum.

"Not likely," the old man contradicted. "Not with his hands tied the way they were. Must have made O'Fallon suffer something fierce, trying to escape and not being able to do it."

The tall, lumbering Concord stage pulled up and the driver jumped down. The local agent began unloading mail pouches while the passengers climbed in.

"You best be goin'," the old man said. He smiled, showing yellowed and cracked teeth. "Cripple Creek's got a real treat in store when you show up, mister. Yes, sir!"

Slocum touched his shirt pocket, where forty dollars in greenbacks rested. It had been all O'Fallon had on him before Slocum had sent him to hell.

The money would get Slocum to Cripple Creek. He swung up and into the coach, settling between the patent medicine salesman and the window.

2

John Slocum settled back and tried to get comfortable on the stagecoach's slick hardwood seat. No matter how he turned, it wasn't possible. When the three span of horses began up the steeper grades, Slocum gave up and tried not to think about it.

His mind wandered, half asleep. He couldn't help but notice the woman across from him. Slocum wondered what possessed a woman of such breeding to go to Cripple Creek. By all accounts, the town was like every other mining camp: rough, harsh, no place for a lady.

She looked more decked out for the opera than for a rugged trip in a battered Concord stage. Her soft brown hair had been neatly tucked under a feather toque. The beige cashmere basque looked fresh and clean for all the traveling she must have done recently. Slocum almost laughed when he saw her dainty opera-heeled shoes. The miner next to her wore high-laced boots that looked capable of stomping through the swiftest-running stream in the Rockies and never leaking.

The brunette responded to Slocum's attention by averting her eyes. She sat with her hands folded in a chaste manner completely out of touch with everything around her.

"Mama," said the twelve-year-old girl seated on her right, "will be we long?"

"No, Kitty, we'll be there before sundown. I know you're tired, but it is only thirty miles more." She lapsed into silence, her cold look silencing the child's questions.

Slocum wondered if the woman's snooty attitude came from having to travel with low-lifes such as him and the miners, or if it meant something else. The girl —Kitty, her mother had called her—seemed comfortable in her surroundings.

One corduroy-clad miner coughed and spat out the window. Slocum turned his head aside in time to keep the gob of tobacco from hitting him. The spittle had gone out the miner's window and in Slocum's.

"Sorry," the man muttered. "Damned stage is no way to travel."

"Going to Cripple Creek to get rich?" Slocum asked.

"Been all over Idaho looking for gold. Decided the Crik is the best chance I'll ever have in this life," the man answered. "Probably end up flat busted, but there's no telling until I try."

"We may end up dead," said the other miner. He shifted on the smooth wood seat and peered out the window. "Road agents all along this route, or so they tell me."

Slocum instinctively checked to see how the other men were armed. The miner across from him had an ancient Colt Dragoon thrust into his belt. If that old pistol were ever fired, it might blow up in the user's hand. Even without close inspection, Slocum saw gnawing islands of rust on the cylinder. The condition of the barrel couldn't be much better. The miner worrying over outlaws didn't have a six-shooter. Slocum thought he might have a derringer in a pocket, but he doubted it.

From the corner of his eye, Slocum looked over the

patent medicine salesman. The mere idea of holding a gun would scare the bejesus out of him.

"Is such violence always necessary?" the woman asked primly. "It never solves anything."

"Ma'am," Slocum said, "I hate to contradict you, but violence *always* solves problems. Try asking anyone face down in the dirt, dead from a bullet in his head."

"Don't be ridiculous," she snapped. "If the man is dead, he cannot answer any question."

"That's right," said Slocum. "The dispute is settled in favor of whoever killed him. Violence does settle conflicts."

The brunette's brown eyes turned hard as she glared at him. Slocum hardly noticed. He leaned back, his mind casting back to the years after he had ridden with Quantrill's Raiders. Slocum had protested the senseless slaughter at Lawrence, Kansas, and had got shot for his trouble. The wound had taken months to heal.

An elbow jostled him. He lifted one eyelid and peered at the traveling salesman. The man fumbled in his bag and pulled out a bottle half filled with amber liquid.

"Doctor Pequod's Elixir for Nerves and Jaundice," the salesman said almost guiltily. He took off the top and knocked back a healthy swig. The pungent odor mingling with the dust inside the coach told Slocum that the magical elixir was more likely rye whiskey.

"Amazing man, Doctor Pequod," Slocum said.

The patent medicine salesman silently held out the bottle. Slocum took a quick nip. He'd been right. The rye burned all the way down his gullet and puddled warmly in his belly. It didn't make the unpleasant traveling conditions go away, but it took the edge off them.

"Thanks. You selling your wares up in Cripple Creek?" he asked as he handed back the bottle. Before answering, the salesman took another healthy slug of the whiskey.

"That I am. Mining camps can be rife with unsanitary conditions. Only the good doctor's products can alleviate the suffering and disease that abounds."

"Disease," the young girl piped up. "Are there dangerous diseases in Cripple Creek?"

"Certainly, young lady," the medicine peddler said earnestly, seeing in her curiosity a possible sale. "Diphtheria. Lockjaw. Consumption. All terrible bad this time of year."

"But the young lady's not going to catch any of that, is she?" Slocum asked. His cold green eyes locked on the peddler's watery blue ones.

"Oh, no, nothing like that. She'll be perfectly fine. Yes, fine. Really, young lady. You have nothing to fear."

"But the miners do?" Kitty asked, her eyes wide and innocent.

"Mining's hard work," said Slocum. "Injuries happen. Hard to take good care of yourself when you're working fifteen hours a day trying to pull all the gold you can from a claim." He smiled. "You're not thinking of becoming a miner, are you?"

Before she could answer, her mother motioned her to silence. The lovely brunette said, "Of course not. Be quiet, Kitty, and leave the gentlemen alone."

"She's no bother," Slocum said.

Heavy silence fell, punctuated only by the creaking of the coach, the clatter of the wheels, and the snapping of leather tack as the six horses pulled the coach.

The woman looked up, startled, when the coach stopped. "What's wrong?" she asked.

"Holdup. Must be a holdup," moaned a miner. He closed his eyes and his lips moved in silent prayer.

The driver opened the door and stuck his head in. "Everybody out for a while. Watering the horses before we take the Shelf road up into the District. Stretch your legs. It's gonna be a long time before you get the chance again."

The two miners jumped out and yawned, stretching mightily. The salesman followed. When Slocum silently offered his help to the woman, she pointedly ignored him. Kitty, however, seemed to appreciate the attention as he swung her over and put her on the ground.

"Thank you," the girl said, smiling. She eyed his gun, thought for a moment, then asked, "Have you ever killed anyone with your pistol, sir?"

"Kitty!" her mother exclaimed. "Sir, I am appalled at her lack of manners. Forgive her."

"No offense taken, ma'am," Slocum said. "After our earlier talk, it's a natural question."

"You have!" cried Kitty. Her wide eyes got wider. She clutched at something tied into a lace handkerchief and fastened at her patent leather belt.

"Don't reckon I'll be shooting anyone today," Slocum said.

"But you would, if it became necessary?" The girl seemed fascinated by him and his worn Colt.

"Where do you hail from?" he asked, changing the topic. Her mother gave him as close to a look of gratitude as he was likely to get from her. "You appear to have traveled a long ways."

"We've come from Kansas City," Kitty told him. "We were staying with Uncle Henry and Aunt Emma until Papa got settled. I'd never ridden on trains before. Or not so that I remember."

"You were pretty young, then, when you took your first train ride?" Slocum asked.

"Oh, yes, sir, very young. We went east from Silver Reef."

Slocum thought on it. "That's in southern Utah. You're coming back home, aren't you?"

"Almost. I don't remember much of it," the girl said solemnly. "Except that there were lots of Mormons who wouldn't do any gold mining."

"Kitty," her mother rebuked sharply. "Their religion doesn't allow them to mine."

The young girl hung her head as if she had said something wrong. "I apologize, sir."

"What for?" asked Slocum, surprised. "It's no moral fault if they don't work in mines."

"My papa thinks it is."

Pieces of a complicated puzzle fell into place for Slocum. The girl's father had ended up in Cripple Creek and had finally hit it big enough to send for his wife and daughter. Somehow, though, Slocum found it hard to believe the woman was a miner's wife. She didn't have the hard-rock look about her. Silver Reef was no genteel, polite society town, either. The Mormons brought a touch of civilization to it, but life was hard in southern Utah. Kansas City society was the place for this woman —not Cripple Creek.

"Everybody back in. We're ready for the steep grades," the driver called. "Don't think we'll have to do it, but be ready to jump out and walk, if the horses get too tired on the hills."

"Walk?" the woman asked, startled. "I thought that—"

"Don't worry your head none about it, ma'am," the driver said. "The men can walk a spell, if need be. You won't have to. A slender little thing like you don't mean spit to these horses. Everybody in!"

This time the brunette allowed Slocum to help her in. Kitty waited patiently for her turn. Slocum hoisted her into the coach and followed. The two miners got in, arguing about road agents.

"They run with Quantrill, I say. Mean sons of bitches. They'd as soon shoot you in the back as look at you."

"Every road agent's run with Quantrill, or so they say," said the other. "Makes 'em sound meaner'n they really are."

The brunette had gone pale at the mention of Quantrill. Slocum understood why, if she had been in Kansas during the War.

"Are there really outlaws on this road?" she asked.

"Probably," said Slocum. "Any road with gold shipments along it is bound to attract highwaymen. But there's no reason to rob a stage going *into* the Cripple

Creek District. No gold on it. The trip back is the one likely to be dangerous."

"No mail delivery, either," said the traveling salesman. "The post office has changed branches so many times, the mail takes months to get through—if ever. The stage isn't carrying any mail and hasn't for several weeks."

"Mama, that means—"

"Quiet, Kitty," her mother interrupted. This brief exchange added to Slocum's guesswork about them. The woman had written repeatedly to her husband and not gotten a reply, so they had come out to investigate firsthand. Or maybe she had written her husband telling him they were coming out and now worried that he did not know—and she was concerned over what she might find on arrival.

The coach lurched as they started up a steep slope that had been blasted from solid rock. Slocum glanced out the window and down a five-hundred-foot cliff. Across from him, Kitty stared at the drop, her mouth open in astonishment. For a flatlander, this part of the Rocky Mountains would be startling.

"Will we make it?" asked the medicine peddler. "The horses seem to be faltering."

"We'll make it," said Slocum. The horses strained but did not weaken. Almost as soon as the words left his mouth, they reached the top of the hill and slowed.

The Concord stopped. For a moment, Slocum wondered what had happened. It wasn't likely that the driver rested the horses. The pull had been hard, but not that hard for the strong team.

"Oh, sweet Jesus, moaned the miner worried most about highwaymen. "We're being robbed!"

"Everyone outside!" came the shouted command. "Now, or I start killing the horses!"

The driver squawked in protest, then joined in telling his passengers to get out.

"No," the brunette said, a gloved hand going to her

mouth. Then she turned to her daughter. The girl fumbled at the lace handkerchief tied to her belt.

"Don't worry," said Slocum. "They can't get too much more than our money." Beside him the peddler took a long draught of his whiskey, then tossed the empty bottle back into his bag.

"Out, damn you all!" cried a road agent. The masked outlaw jerked open the door and reached. He grabbed a handful of corduroy and yanked, sending a miner to the ground. "The rest of you, hurry it up! We ain't got all day!"

"They all rode with Quantrill," moaned the miner as he pulled himself off the ground. "They'll kill us all, just for the practice."

The outlaws were more concerned with Slocum when they saw the Colt in his holster. One with a shotgun motioned. Slocum carefully laid the weapon on the ground. The miner carrying the rusty Dragoon tossed his down, not caring about any damage the rocky ground might do upon impact.

"That's the way we like to see 'em," the outlaw leader said. "Nice and cooperative. Saves us having to blow holes in your worthless hides!"

"We're all gonna die," the miner moaned. "They all rode with Quantrill and they're gonna kill us all!"

The leader snapped around when he heard this. His hand moved slightly, bringing his shotgun around and ready to kill. He relaxed when he looked at the cowering miner. Then he tensed when his eyes locked with Slocum's.

A spark of recognition passed between them. Slocum went icy cold inside. This road agent *had* been with Quantrill. He couldn't remember his name, but he remembered the set of his body, the long, white scar running across his forehead, and the eyes. Always the eyes. They carried a kill-craziness that Slocum had seen too often among the Redlegs.

"Only the money," said the leader. "Nothing else."

"But . . ." one outlaw started to protest. The roar of the shotgun as it discharged drowned out the rest of the sentence.

"Do as you're told or the next barrel takes your filthy head off."

Slocum glanced at the woman. She had turned white with shock. Kitty's actions puzzled him, though. She popped something into her mouth.

"Everything into the sack," said the outlaw leader. "Hold back on us and we'll toss you over the side." He gestured in the direction of the sheer cliff. "Won't be till spring thaw before you even hit bottom."

Slocum passed over the wad of greenbacks he had taken from Kid O'Fallon. Although it was all the money he had, it didn't pain him to see it go. Blood money never brought good luck.

"And what about you, little lady?" the outlaw asked, stopping in front of the brunette. "What you got hidden?"

Slocum tensed. The outlaw leader bellowed, "Leave her alone. Just the money." The leader dismounted and came over. He stood and stared at Slocum, as if making sure of his identification. Slocum never blinked or changed expression.

"She with you?" the outlaw asked.

"We're traveling together." Slocum was glad the woman had the good sense to keep her mouth shut. A denial now took her out from under what little protection he afforded her by having ridden with this outlaw for even a few weeks many years back.

"Let her be," the outlaw said. He turned, then spun when the other road agent grabbed Kitty.

"She's got something in her mouth. She's hiding it!"

"Don't—" the woman started. Slocum restrained her.

The leader grabbed Kitty's nose and tugged upward. On the girl's tongue rested a silver dollar.

"Look at that. A cartwheel. Where did you get it?"

"My uncle. He gave it to me before we left Kansas City. You're not going to take it, are you? It's all I have."

"Take it? Hell, no. You're a brave one. Here." The outlaw reached into his vest pocket and withdrew another silver dollar. "Put this with the one your uncle gave you." He looked up and saw that the others had finished their thievery. Anything of value had been stripped from the coach.

"Get along now, and don't go thinking about a posse. We own these hills," he told the driver.

"Wouldn't do no good," the driver said. "The sheriff in the District has got more to do than he can handle."

The outlaws laughed harshly, mounted, and motioned for the passengers to get back into the coach. When they were inside, the road agents began firing. The team bucked and tried to run. It required the driver's full attention to get them quieted and to keep the coach from taking the sharp turns in the road too fast.

"I knew it," moaned the miner who had been afraid of outlaws. "I knew it. My entire stake is gone! All gone! What am I gonna do now?"

"Same as everyone else," grumbled the other miner. He crossed his arms and looked sullen. "I even lost my damned gun."

Slocum nodded. Leaving his on the ground was a major blow, too. Money came and went. It was hard finding a six-shooter as good as that Colt had been.

"Thank you, sir," the woman said, "for what you did back there."

"What the hell did he do?" demanded the peddler. "He ponied up his money just like everyone else."

The brunette ignored him. She was still pale, but touches of color had returned to her cheeks. Slocum might have seen a more lovely woman, but he couldn't remember when or where.

"Thank you," she said simply.

"Mama," Kitty spoke up. "He kept us from being robbed, didn't he?"

The woman whispered for several seconds. Kitty smiled shyly, then whispered back. Slocum was starting to ignore them when the woman's face turned pale with shock again.

"Kitty, no!"

"Yes, Mama. May I return it to him?"

Slocum frowned when the girl reached into the folds of her skirt and pulled out his Colt. Kitty handed it to him, her small fingers barely able to circle its butt.

"You picked it up," he said in surprise. "That was a very brave thing to do. And very foolish. Those men were killers."

Kitty smiled at his praise, then shyly looked away.

He settled the Colt back into its holster, comfortable now that its weight again rested on his hip. The girl had been foolish and courageous. Slocum smiled to himself. He reckoned that she came by those traits honestly— from her mother.

3

John Slocum shook the dust from his hat and brushed himself off the best he could after he dropped to the main street of Cripple Creek. He looked up and down the rutted, muddy street and had the impression that he had seen it a hundred times before. One gold rush town looked much like another.

He picked up Kitty and lifted her down from the coach, then held out his hand for her mother. The woman frowned slightly, then allowed him to help her. The way she reacted to him made him think he had tangled with a skunk.

From the box, the driver yelled to the small crowd gathered, "Anybody seen the sheriff? We been held up on the road, about ten miles back, just above Phantom Canyon."

Most of the people in the crowd on the boardwalk looked bored. One shouted back, "The sheriff's quit. He staked a claim on the other side of Battle Mountain and is working it. Won't be long before another man comes up from Denver, though."

"Like hell," grumbled the driver. "Better'n a month, and I'll be the sorry son of a bitch who has to get him here. Shit." The man dropped down and began tending his horses.

"That's all?" asked the woman, startled. "There's not going to be a posse formed to go after those ruffians?"

"Doubt it, ma'am," said the driver. "We weren't robbed of anything important."

"I beg your pardon! A crime was committed. Doesn't that matter to the citizens of Cripple Creek?"

"Reckon it might, but only when it's their money being stolen. You came out all right, thanks to this here fellow."

"It's the principle!" The brunette stamped her daintily shod foot and spattered mud onto the hem of her skirt.

"Getting killed for your principles means a damn sight more when it's your money involved," the driver said. He finished unhitching his team and began leading the horses away in pairs.

"What a barbaric place," she muttered.

"Ma'am, my name's John Slocum. Don't think we've been properly introduced." Slocum found himself on the receiving end of an icy cold stare.

"Go on, Mama." Kitty tugged at her mother's dress.

"I am Mina Barclay," she said primly. She held out a hand. Slocum didn't know whether she expected him to shake it or kiss it. He took it lightly, then tipped his hat. A tiny shower of dust came off it.

"And I'm Kitty Barclay. We're here to find my papa. You wouldn't know him, would you, Mr. Slocum?"

"That's doubtful," Slocum answered. "This is my first time in the Cripple Creek District. What's his name? If I come across him, I'd certainly let you know."

"Jonathan Barclay," Kitty said before her mother could hush her.

"I'll keep an eye out for him." Slocum hesitated. Mina Barclay looked around impatiently—or did he detect more than a hint of uneasiness in her? "Can I help you ladies find a place to stay? I don't have any money left, but there's always something that can be arranged."

"I suspect a man like you would know how to get by without money," Mina Barclay said caustically.

"Mama, please, he's just being polite." The girl started scanning the faces around them, looking for her father. The empty, stricken expression matched that of her mother. Wherever Jonathon Barclay was, he wasn't here to greet his family.

The two miners had left, but the patent medicine peddler spoke up, saying, "You'd best find something in a hurry. It doesn't pay to be out on Myers Avenue after dark. Not if you have refined senses."

Slocum looked up and down Myers Avenue and understood what the peddler meant. This was the middle of the red-light district. The whorehouses only now stirred with life. In another hour they would be doing a roaring business.

"Where's a good hotel for the ladies?" he asked the peddler.

"The Continental down the street a ways. Maybe the Palace over on Second Street."

"We can find our own lodging, thank you." Mina Barclay took up her bags and gestured to Kitty to do likewise. They started up the street, into the heart of the red-light district. Kitty gave one glance back at Slocum, then turned and hurried after her mother.

"What's in that direction?" Slocum asked.

"Poverty Gulch. If they keep walking far enough, they can get to Carbonate Hill, where some miners' shacks are. Those that can afford shacks. Most live in tents."

The peddler settled his clothing and brushed the travel dust off. "I'd better get to work. I got to sell ten bottles of Doctor Pequod's if I want a meal and a place to sleep." With that, the peddler went off to find a small crowd desperately needing protection from scurvy, dropsy, smallpox, and the ague.

Slocum searched through his own pockets and found a single dime. It wasn't much, but it would buy him a shot of cheap whiskey. He picked up his gear and set off along Myers Avenue.

To his right and up a hill rose a street lined with posh

houses—those who had found their gold. He smiled when he saw a crudely lettered sign proclaiming this to be Golden Hill Avenue. What else would it be called?

The wealth this single street represented contrasted sharply with Poverty Gulch and the desperate miners he had seen near the stage depot. He continued walking. The Roberts Grocery had closed for the night or he might have traded his dime for some decent food. Farther on, two men still struggled in the back room of a laundry to run a printing press. *The Weekly Crusher* had been lettered above the door leading to the room.

Slocum walked on, taking in the sights of the boom town. He came to the end of the road and dropped his gear. He didn't cotton to the idea of sleeping under the stars, not when October winds blew with increasing chill off Pikes Peak. Still, he saw no other choice.

He looked back, thought of Mina Barclay and her daughter, then sighed. He hefted his gear and started back. Mrs. Barclay didn't want his help. Maybe she had found her husband and didn't need it. But he couldn't get the woman's stricken look out of his mind. She had expected to find Jonathan Barclay waiting for her, and he had not been there.

Cripple Creek was a different world from Kansas City.

Slocum stopped outside Crapper Jack's Saloon. Inside a brawl raged. One man stumbled through the swinging doors, blood gushing from a cut on his forehead. Another roared and followed him into the street. Slocum stepped aside and let them settle their differences. Much of the crowd had poured outside to watch. Slocum forced his way through the onlookers cheering on their personal favorite and dropped his gear in the corner where he could keep an eye on it.

He had been robbed once today. Twice would make him powerful mad.

He bellied up to the bar and dropped his dime on the highly polished wood. "What'll this buy me a shot of?" he asked.

"You just get into the Crik?" the barkeep asked. The man's heavy mustache twitched, the ends bouncing around as he smiled.

"I was on the stage."

"You was robbed. Gus already came through telling about it."

"The driver?" Slocum guessed. The barkeep nodded. "Don't have to tell you, then, that this dime's all you're likely to see from me."

"Crapper Jack won't like it, but screw him. The old bastard's never been down on his luck in his life." The barkeep poured a stiff shot into a beer mug. "Can't give you more'n that."

"I surely do thank you." Slocum tipped the amber fluid back and let it trickle down his throat. It hit him like a blow. "Powerful stuff."

"We make it here in Cripple Creek," the barkeep told him. "Got our own brewery, too. Zang's Brewery, down by the Masonic Hall."

Slocum looked over his shoulder when the crowd drifted back in. The way the barkeep moved away when the bear of a man in the center of the crowd came to the bar told Slocum this had to be Crapper Jack, the saloon owner.

"That ought to take care of that sneaky son of a bitch," Crapper Jack declared. He had been the one who had hit the miner over the head with a bottle and opened the nasty cut Slocum had seen on his way in.

The men on either side of the bar owner bobbed their heads in agreement. Slocum noticed that Crapper Jack didn't offer to buy them drinks.

The sudden hush that fell brought Slocum around so that his back was to a wall and his hand rested near the butt of his Colt.

"Where is he? Where's Crapper Jack?" The miner who had been thrown out only a few minutes before stumbled into the saloon, blood flowing from the spiderweb of cuts on his forehead. Crapper Jack had done a good job of turning the man's face into raw meat, but he had not broken the man's spirit.

The crowd parted like the Red Sea and left only empty space between Crapper Jack and the miner who carried an axe handle.

"Ain't you had enough yet, McKinnie?" the saloon owner asked. "I don't want to teach you another lesson. Go on home and sober up."

"You stinking thief. You robbed me of my money. The poker game was crooked." The miner came forward, heavily dragging one leg behind. Slocum wondered if Crapper Jack had stomped the leg, too. Probably. The bar owner looked to be one mean hombre.

Crapper Jack roared and charged. McKinnie grunted —and did what he did best. The axe handle rose and fell in a powerful arc that shattered Crapper Jack's head like a watermelon. Blood and brains spattered out on the stunned onlookers.

If McKinnie had left it at that, he might have walked out and no one would have much cared. But he went berserk. Swinging the axe handle, he struck whoever was closest, then went to work on the chairs, tables, and bottles.

Slocum would have been content to let the man rage on, but he stood between McKinnie and the back bar.

The miner roared and tried to crush Slocum's head the way he had Crapper Jack's. Slocum didn't think consciously; he acted. He ducked inside the arc of that deadly axe handle and caught McKinnie's wrist in a powerful grip. The miner grunted and jerked free. He was stronger than Slocum by a mite.

Slocum was in no mood to fight. His left fist came down in a short arc that ended on the side of McKinnie's head. The miner stumbled back. Slocum moved in, fists going for the midsection. Punch after punch landed on a rock-hard gut. When he saw that he wasn't doing any serious damage to the miner, Slocum yanked out his Colt.

McKinnie was still off-balance when Slocum swung

the Colt with all his strength and landed the barrel on the top of the miner's head. McKinnie went down as if all his bones had turned to mush.

"Go on, mister. Finish him off," called someone from the crowd. The cold look Slocum shot him quieted the crowd's bloodlust. He stepped over McKinnie's unconscious form and quietly asked, "Can I have another drink—on the house?"

"Sure, mister, sure, anything," the barkeep said. He had turned pale when Crapper Jack had been bashed over the head. He had pulled out his own weapon, a long, slender bag loaded with sand, but he seemed to know that he would have stood no chance against McKinnie's berserk rage.

"Give him the entire bottle. He's earned it," said a man, forcing his way through the crowd. He glanced over at Crapper Jack's corpse and made a wry face. "Always told him he'd lose his head in this business."

"You look to be in charge," observed Slocum. He tried to size up the man who had given him the free whiskey. Under other circumstances, Slocum would have ignored the man. Nothing unusual about him stood out. The green-dyed linen coat he wore had seen better days—a long time back. The brocade vest showed spots of liquor and sweat. The chain dangling from the watch pocket gleamed green in places where the plated gold had worn off to reveal base metal. The cloth trousers had shiny spots where the man did most of his work, and the boots needed polishing.

A bulge in a vest pocket might be a derringer, Slocum thought. And the .32 caliber pistol in the crossdraw holster had seen heavy use. From the man's pale eyes Slocum guessed that there would be no remorse when he did use the six-shooter. Quick fingers dextrously worked a coin up and down.

"You a gambler?" Slocum asked, choosing the most likely profession that fit everything about the man.

"You might say that." He ran his hands through greasy black hair and looked up, as if seeing the saloon for the first time. "Crapper Jack's is a lousy name for the place. What would you call it?"

"Not mine to name," Slocum said.

"With that son of a bitch dead, I reckon it *is* mine. Oscar Jacobson is the name." He thrust out his hand. Slocum shook it. No calluses. Jacobson did no hard manual labor, unlike most of the patrons in the saloon. If Slocum was any judge, Jacobson didn't even use his pistol much. The softness of his hand was almost repulsive.

Jacobson looked Slocum over and nodded slowly. "I like your looks. You handled McKinnie real good."

"You saw?"

"I was just coming in. I'd been down the street at the Nugget Saloon. They're still watering down their whiskey."

Oscar Jacobson leaned forward, both elbows on the bar. He stared into the mirror behind the bar and watched those in the room. They milled around, some leaving, others moving as far away from Crapper Jack's body as they could. No one ventured close to McKinnie. The miner still lay on the floor, out like a light.

"You need a job." The way Jacobson said it was a statement, not a question.

"If you heard about the coach being robbed, you know I lost my stake," said Slocum.

"You handled things *real* good. You willing to use your six-shooter, if the need arises?"

"I've used it when I had to," Slocum said cautiously. He wasn't going to hire on as this man's paid killer.

"You look to be the sort of man who could keep the peace within these walls. I'll pay you five dollars a day."

"Not much to risk your life for," Slocum said. McKinnie stirred on the floor. "Drunk miners don't care who they kill."

"Five a day, plus privileges. Ask anybody. That's a good deal."

Slocum glanced at the barkeep, who nodded slightly.

Knowing that the barkeep had no real love for Jacobson convinced Slocum that five dollars and "privileges," whatever that meant, was worthwhile pay.

"All I do is keep them from busting up the place?" he asked.

"And each other," added Jacobson. "Hate to see them get their faces smashed up. Hard to drink that way, and revenues go down while they're recovering."

Slocum laughed, then wondered if Jacobson joked. He might actually think this way.

"Crapper Jack's," Jacobson said, letting the name slide off his tongue like a drop of oil. "A name change is in order. How's the Golconda Saloon sound?"

"The mother lode," muttered the barkeep. "Yeah, Mr. Jacobson. I like it. Got a sound to it, all rich and nice."

"Then it's the Golconda. See that the sign gets repainted tomorrow morning, first thing."

"What about your former partner?" Slocum pointed to the corpse in the middle of the saloon.

"He can rot in hell for all I care." Jacobson stepped past Slocum and grabbed McKinnie by the front of his corduroy jacket. He shook the miner until the man's eyes opened. "You killed Jack, you mangy cayoose. I ought to see you strung up."

"Mr. Jacobson. He . . . he got me all riled."

"See that he gets a decent burial up in Pisgah Graveyard and I won't send Mr. Slocum after you." Jacobson moved to one side to let McKinnie see his new employee. "You understand?"

"Yes, sir."

"Get him out of here before he starts to smell up the place worse'n it is now." Jacobson dragged McKinnie over and released him next to the body. The miner got to his feet and began dragging Crapper Jack outside.

"Glad that's taken care of," said Jacobson. "Reckon you might want an advance on your salary."

"Reckon I want to be paid for today's work," Slocum said. "No reason I should work for nothing."

"Wasn't a full day," said Jacobson. "Ah, hell, here." He dropped a five-dollar greenback on the bar and slapped Slocum on the back. "You're just what the Golconda Saloon needs. Yes, sir." Laughing, Jacobson turned and left. Slocum scooped up the bill and tucked it in his shirt pocket.

"You don't much like him, do you?" Slocum asked the bartender.

"We both work for him." The barkeep polished the spot where Jacobson had leaned as if this would remove all trace of the man's presence.

Slocum looked around. The newly named Golconda was quiet. The few miners remaining seemed intent on losing themselves in their whiskey or beer and not bothering anyone.

"It's been a long day. I'm going to find a place to stay. Any recommendations?"

"The Continental is down the street. The Palace is over on Second. The National's not too bad. Those are it. Nowhere else to stay. And you might have trouble at all of them. This is a boom town and sleeping space is at a premium."

Slocum understood that all too well. He said good night and left, his gear weighing him down more than it had before. He was nearing the end of his rope. A good night's sleep and a hearty breakfast would put him back in the pink.

He headed for the Continental, passing the whorehouses. He slowed, then stopped when he saw two dark figures huddling in an alley. Something familiar about them made him walk closer.

"Mama, it's getting cold," Kitty said. The smaller shape shivered.

"Quiet, dear. I know. We'll be all right." Mina Barclay put her arm around her daughter and pulled her close.

"This looks to be a good way of freezing to death," said Slocum. "The winds coming off the Rockies this time of year bring along a fair amount of snow."

"Who? Oh, it's you, Mr. Slocum."

"Why are you in this alley?"

"None of the hotels had any space," Kitty piped up.

"None had room for someone without money," Slocum corrected.

"We tried St. Peter's Church over on Golden but there was no room for us there," said Mina.

"Miners were sleeping everywhere," cut in Kitty. "The reverend said that it's even worse up in Poverty Gulch. Why, some of those men even sleep in Pisgah Graveyard!"

"Were the hotels full-up, or just not renting to indigents?"

"The Continental had a room, or so the clerk said. He seemed a kindly sort, but he would lose his job if he let us stay without paying."

Slocum wondered what else the clerk had said to Mrs. Barclay. From her tone, he had offered a trade she had been unwilling to accept.

"I might be able to help, ma'am, if you'd like me to try."

"No, Mr. Slocum. You've done enough for us this day."

"Mama, please, I'm *cold!*"

Her daughter's plaintive tone and the sudden drop in temperature convinced her. Mina Barclay nodded curtly. Slocum helped her to her feet. Together they went to the Continental. The clerk looked up from behind the counter. His face went pasty when he saw Slocum.

"I understand you have a room to rent."

"You . . . you're the one who dropped McKinnie."

"News travels fast."

"Ain't much else to do in the District but gossip," the clerk said. He swallowed hard, his Adam's apple bobbing like a stone caught in his throat.

"Then you know I got a job working for Oscar Jacobson. I—and Mr. Jacobson—would look kindly on it if you could find a room for these ladies."

"Yes, sir, but the money. I can't let them have it without pay. No matter what."

Slocum pulled the greenback from his pocket and dropped it on the counter. "Does this cover the room?"

"No, sir. Rooms are ten a night. Everything's expensive in Cripple Creek."

Slocum did not doubt it. Gold towns combined the best and worst features. Immense amounts of money could be made overnight—and the expenses matched it.

"Mr. Jacobson can vouch for me, if necessary. I'm good for the other five. You'll have it tomorrow."

"I . . . I think that will be all right, sir." The clerk pushed the register across to Mina Barclay. She signed her name and Kitty's.

"Thank you, Mr. Slocum. I'm not sure when we can repay you, but rest assured that we will. When Jonathan arrives, we will have the wherewithal."

"Don't worry about it," Slocum said. "Get a good night's sleep." He tipped his hat and headed out. He turned up his collar at the wintry October blast that met him. The money he had intended to get him lodging and food had been well spent, he felt. But he was back to being flat broke.

"The miners sleep in the cemetery, Kitty said. Leastways, if I freeze to death there, they won't have far to drag my corpse." He put his head down and walked into the wind, heading along Myers Avenue until he got to the Pisgah Graveyard.

His bedroll did much to keep out the cold, but Slocum still slept fitfully. He couldn't help worrying about Mina Barclay and her daughter.

4

John Slocum stirred and moaned as he tried to straighten his arms. They seemed frozen to his body. He rolled onto his back and stared into the faint light of dawn. Grays and pinks swirled around the horizon, outlining the thrusting dark peaks of the Rockies. He blinked the sleep from his eyes and sat up. The ground in the cemetery had been colder than he would have thought possible for early October, but he had to remember winter came quick and vicious at this altitude. The daytime sun always promised warm nights — and lied.

He began rubbing circulation back into his arms and legs and pulled himself free of his bedroll. It would have been better spending the night in a warm bed in the Continental, but he thought his money had been well spent. Mina Barclay seemed like a babe in the woods. If it had been just that, Slocum might not have bothered with her. But she was damned pretty, and her daughter was feisty.

Slocum smiled, remembering the way she had tried to hide her silver dollar from the robbers.

The memory of the robbers turned Slocum colder inside than out. He couldn't remember the leader's name, but he remembered the man. So many had ridden with

Quantrill toward the end of the War that Slocum had given up trying to recall their names. They were all the same: killers.

The large white scar that crossed the road agent's forehead stuck in Slocum's mind, though. He had a score to settle with this former ally. Forty dollars wasn't much, but it was all Slocum had in the world—and he had killed Kid O'Fallon to get even that much—

He looked around Pisgah Graveyard and paused. It looked as if the dead were rising from their resting places. All around him miners stirred, yawned and belched, and began packing up their gear. Not a one would strike it rich, Slocum knew. But the dream drove them on.

In the distance he heard heavy machinery working. That had to be the Independence Mine up on Battle Mountain, a big operation run by a mining syndicate out of Denver. The other sound Slocum heard demanded immediate attention. His belly complained about the lack of food.

He rolled his blankets and hefted his gear for the walk back into town. As he walked he considered asking Oscar Jacobson if he could sleep behind the bar. It had to be more comfortable than the center of a cemetery. Slocum had briefly thought on it the night before and had decided not to bother his new employer. Better to appear aloof than needy. Unless he missed his guess, Jacobson wasn't the charitable kind who responded well to weakness in his employees—and he'd have to see it as weakness that Slocum had already spent his pay, and on what.

Slocum went into the Golconda Saloon, surprised to see the new sign already in place. The barkeep polished the glasses and didn't even look up as Slocum leaned against the bar.

"Didn't take Jacobson long to get the sign in place," Slocum said.

"Son of a bitch had it out back."

Slocum said nothing. He wondered if Jacobson had

put the miner up to killing Crapper Jack. That was a mighty easy way of getting rid of an unwanted partner. Who was to say that miners didn't get drunk and go a little crazy? Especially in a place like Cripple Creek.

"You want some breakfast, go in the back and rustle it up for yourself. Just don't burn the damn place down."

Slocum silently left. The barkeep's foul mood had carried over from last night. He didn't care for their new employer one whit, but jobs other than mining were scarce. Slocum found a wood stove and laid a fire. The food was sparse but he was hungry enough to eat the south end of a northbound mule. A rasher of bacon had been stored outside; Slocum scraped off the mold and dropped some of the meat into an iron skillet. Some bread and a dipper of water from the well out back finished off the meal.

The barkeep came in and dropped into a chair across from Slocum. "You don't have much to do until the afternoon. Jacobson wants you to keep the place quiet. Some of the poor sots actually liked Jack and might want to stir up trouble over his killing."

"Did McKinnie have a grudge against Crapper Jack?"

The barkeep's eyes narrowed. "Why do you ask?"

"Just thinking how convenient it is having an entire saloon given over to you because your partner's head collides with an axe handle."

"Don't let Jacobson hear you sayin' things like that. Might be true. Might not be. Just don't let him hear you."

Slocum had seen Crapper Jack. The man had been built like one of the massive peaks of the Rockies. Oscar Jacobson had nowhere near the size or muscle, but Slocum got the impression that he was a damned sight meaner and a lot trickier.

"He won't hear a word out of me," said Slocum. "I need a job. Any dispute with a former owner doesn't concern me none."

The barkeep nodded, his mustache twitching. "Your gear'll be safe back here."

Slocum looked around the small kitchen. To the left was the storage room with kegs of whiskey and beer. To the right was the saloon's main room.

"Ever have trouble with thieving from the storeroom?" he asked.

"You need a place to sleep? Hell, five dollars a day is a princely sum, but it don't buy spit in the District." The barkeep looked around as if he were afraid of being overheard. "Look, I got a deal going that can't be beat. I slip something into some of the richer miners' drinks. I ain't got no one to finish 'em off like I had."

Slocum understood the situation at the Golconda more fully now. The barkeep and Crapper Jack had been in business for themselves, cutting out Oscar Jacobson. The barkeep drugged the miners and then Crapper Jack robbed them.

The man saw Slocum's expression. "Hell, they don't mind none. We give 'em more than any other place in town. They think of it as an extra service charge. I took in as much as fifty dollars a night. Look, it's good money."

Slocum guessed that the amount was double that. "What'd be my cut?"

The sudden shrewd look confirmed Slocum's suspicions. "I'm a right generous man. I'd cut you in for, say, a quarter. That'd put an extra ten, fifteen dollars a night into your pocket."

"I'll think on it." Slocum had ideas of his own on how to make money off the miners—and not have them coming after him with axe handles. "I'm going to look around Cripple Creek."

"Hey, Slocum," the barkeep called out. "We never been introduced proper-like. The name's Haggerty." Slocum shook hands with the barkeep. When he closed the back door behind him, he wiped his hand on his shirt. Some men carried clean dirt from hard work on their hands. Slocum never minded that. Haggerty carried filth and blood on his, even if you couldn't see it.

Slocum circled the Golconda, made sure that no one saw him, then ducked under the pilings holding the building off the ground. In the dark, dank crawl space, Slocum worked his way toward the center of the saloon. Overhead he heard the measured tread of boots. Peering up through the cracks in the wood planking, he saw Jacobson. What the Golconda's owner said to Haggerty got muffled by the wood, but Slocum didn't much care.

He looked down at the muck. He ran his hands through it, then rubbed his fingers together. A slow smile crossed his lips. The gritty feel came from gold dust. The drunk miners dropped their pokes or carelessly spilled dust when paying for their drinks or gambling debts. Some slipped between the boards and ended up under the saloon.

With a little work, Slocum could make much more than the paltry amount offered by Haggerty for robbing the customers.

Satisfied, Slocum backed out from under the Golconda. He stood back and wiped off the mud, smiling even more broadly now. The saloon had been wellnamed. The mother lode. And it would be, for him.

Slocum walked back toward the stage depot, thinking he might catch sight of Mina Barclay. He found the driver, Gus, sitting on the boardwalk. The man spat accurately, hitting a crawling insect on the rough-hewn planks. Gus looked up when he saw Slocum.

"Howdy," he said. "You thinkin' on goin' back to Colorado Springs? Fare's double. You'll have to pay three dollars, in advance."

"I'll stay a while," Slocum said. "You get held up often?"

"Too damn often," Gus said. He spat again. "Owner of the line is too damn cheap to hire a guard." The driver looked at Slocum and then said, "I'll let you ride back to the Springs for free if you go along as shotgun."

Slocum laughed. He had heard of suicidal proposals before. This one topped them all. "You must be going back with gold dust."

"Didn't say that," Gus said. The sour expression on his face told Slocum that he was. Probably not much or the line would provide a guard, but enough to make the driver uneasy.

"Got a job at the Golconda as bouncer."

"Figured you for that kind," the driver said. Without another word, he heaved himself to his feet and walked off. Slocum watched him vanish into the depot, which doubled as a lunchroom.

"There he is, Mama," came a familiar voice.

"Hush, now, child. Don't go bothering him."

Slocum turned to see Mina Barclay and Kitty behind him. "Good morning, ma'am," he said. "Were the hotel accommodations to your liking?"

"Oh, Mr. Slocum, there were bugs as big as my finger," Kitty exclaimed. "They crawled all over everything. Mama said that—"

"Hush," Mina said sharply. "The room lacked certain cleanliness, Mr. Slocum, but that is to be expected in a place such as Cripple Creek."

"Reckon so. You having any luck finding your husband?"

"Word has been sent to him on our claim, Mr. Slocum. He is to be in town this evening to pick us up. You shall have your money back at that time."

"No hurry," he said. "Get yourself settled in, then we can see about repayment."

"Where'd you sleep, Mr. Slocum?" asked Kitty. "You look a fright!"

"You'd better go with your mama," he said. "She seems itching to be somewhere else. Good day, ma'am," he said, tipping his hat. He watched as Mina Barclay almost dragged her daughter along to get her away from bad influences. They had a heap of learning to do before they found a niche in Cripple Creek, he thought.

Slocum spent the morning walking the streets, going from the rich section of Golden Avenue to the bare subsistence of Poverty Gulch. Most miners were too poor to afford fancy clapboard shacks. They lived in tents, on some of which Slocum made out the Confederate markings. During the War, these had been inadequate. This many years later, they were almost worse than nothing at all between the miners and the elements.

He looked up and saw the sun beginning to slip prematurely behind the tall peaks to the west. Slocum turned back toward the Golconda, thinking he might rustle up some more food before starting to work. On the steps in front of the saloon, he saw a mountain of a man bending forward. Then a slender arm reached around the miner and ineffectually struck him.

"Don't go sayin' no, little darlin'," the miner said. "I ain't got any gold dust, but you can bet that my credit's good. I'll pay you when I can. I love you."

Slocum walked around the man and saw that he held a woman pinned to the planking, one meaty hand over her mouth. She struggled, but the man's strength was too much.

"Pardon me," Slocum said, moving so that the man would have to turn slightly to see him. "What are you doing with her?"

"Huh?" The man-mountain turned. "This ain't none of your business. This is between me and Betsy." The man's hand slipped off the woman's painted mouth.

"This son of a bitch is trying to rape me!"

The miner laughed harshly. "How can you rape a whore? Hell, Betsy here likes me."

"Can't pay?"

"He's stone broke!" the woman snapped. Slocum saw that, for all her bravado, fear etched itself onto her pretty features. Her makeup had been smeared by the man's greasy, dirty hand and her hair was tangled. Her dress had been freshly laundered before the miner had pinned her.

"Can't pay, can't play," Slocum said, moving a little

further around. The miner twisted to follow his action.
When he did, Slocum kicked as hard as he could. The
toe of his boot landed squarely in the center of the
miner's chest, knocking him off the woman.

Before the miner could recover, Slocum moved in. A
second kick caught the miner in the belly. Slocum might
as well have been kicking a granite cliff. The miner
roared and tried to get to his feet. Slocum kicked an arm
the size of a large tree trunk out from under the miner.
The man grunted and fell face down onto the boardwalk.

"Get out of here," Slocum told the woman.

"The hell I will. You can't handle him alone."

Slocum put all the power he could into the rabbit
punch that landed on the back of the man's neck. This
stunned the miner. Slocum winced. His fist hurt from
the blow but he didn't think he'd broken any bones. He
went back to his first attack. He kicked again, his boot
aimed for the miner's square jaw. The man's head
snapped back and he sank forward, as if sleeping.

"Mister, I never saw anything like that before. He
never had a chance," Betsy said in awe.

Slocum rubbed his hand. The miner had had more
than a chance. If he'd been able to get up, Slocum
would have spent the rest of eternity in Pisgah Graveyard rather than just one night.

"Why'd you bother savin' me like that?" Eyes as
blue as Colorado cornflowers stared at him. "Nobody
around the District much cares what happens to a
whore."

"Excuse me. I got to get to work." Slocum grabbed
under the miner's arms and began dragging him in the
direction of the Nugget Saloon. Let him wake up there.
He might not remember where he'd been cold-cocked.

Betsy stood in the door of the Golconda when Slocum got back. She said, "I just talked with Haggerty.
He said you're the new bouncer. You surely do take
your job serious. I work upstairs."

"Then you're part of my job," Slocum said.

"You didn't know that when you got that galoot off me." Betsy paused for a moment, then smiled widely. "I think I'm gonna like bein' part of your job." She looked around, then said in a whisper, "Why don't you be part of my job? Jacobson ain't around to complain about it."

"Suppose I ought to check out the cribs," Slocum said. "That's part of the job that Jacobson never mentioned."

Betsy smiled even more broadly and spun, her skirts flaring as she flounced off. Slocum watched the way she put a hitch in her gitalong—and it was meant just for him. No customers had come into the saloon yet. Haggerty was in the back room watering down the bottles of whiskey before bringing them out. And it had been a powerful long time since Slocum had been with a woman.

He followed Betsy up the stairs and into a room hardly wide enough for his shoulders. On the floor a thin pallet had been spread.

"It ain't much, but I try to keep it clean. Not like some of the others. And Jacobson don't care one way or the other, as long as he gets his cut." Betsy stopped talking and just stood, looking at Slocum. "You're even better-looking than I thought—and that's a considerable amount."

Slocum found his mouth occupied with something better than talking. Betsy kissed him with a fervor that took away his breath. Then he found himself returning it.

She broke off, panting. "I knew you were a gentlemen when you stopped Tiny from having his way with me. But I'm beginning to think there's more to you than that."

"There's one way of seeing," he said. He unbuckled his gunbelt and hung it on the single nail driven into the wall. Slocum couldn't get to the buttons on his shirt in time. Betsy got there first. Her nimble fingers did more than unbutton. She caressed, then dragged her fingernails across his bare chest in a way that excited him more than he could put words to.

She bent forward and kissed his chest, working down slowly.

Slocum gasped when she got his denims unbuttoned and pulled his hardening length out. He sagged back against a wall when her eager lips engulfed him. Her tongue worked miracles all over him.

"You surely do know how to thank a fellow," he said.

Betsy turned her face upward, her blue eyes shining. She did not answer. Her mouth was occupied. Her fingers worked around and cupped his rear. With a bit of tugging she worked his denims down.

"This can get complicated," he said, wiggling around in the narrow crib. He sat down fully on the floor and let the woman pull his trousers off. Then his boots followed.

"This is hardly fair," he said. "You've still got all your clothes on."

"So do something about it," she challenged.

He did.

His fingers worked into the neckline of her dress. Gentle outward pressure caused the buttons to come undone one by one. When he came to the satin ties, Betsy was too anxious to let him awkwardly undo them. She stripped off the last of the ties and wriggled free of her corset.

The twin mounds bobbing gently in the dimly lit room set Slocum's heart pounding even faster.

"Don't just look," she said. "Take them. They're your reward for saving me."

He reached out. Betsy shoved her chest forward and he found both hands filled with warm, firm breasts. His thumbs and forefingers gripped the nipples and squeezed. It was the woman's turn to moan softly. She closed her eyes and arched her back. This shoved her bosom even harder into Slocum's hands.

"Don't be gentle. You can do anything you want," she said, her words coming between short gasps for breath. Her eyes opened. They had begun to glaze with lust. "Oh, how I want you!" she exclaimed.

Slocum bent forward and licked over the turgid nipples. He felt the frenzied beating of her heart through those tiny nubbins of flesh. Squeezing harder brought deeper moans from the woman. She eased back until she fully reclined.

Betsy began struggling to get free of her skirt. Slocum started to reach down and help.

She grabbed a handful of hair on either side of his head and held him firmly. "Don't you dare! You keep doing what you're doing. I love it!"

Slocum smiled and returned to his succulent feast. His lips sucked and pulled at the coppery nubs. He began kneading the fleshy mounds as if they were dough. Betsy gave a long, deep shudder that shook her entire body. "So good," she sighed. "I wish they were all this good to me."

"It can get better," he said.

"Prove it!"

Slocum felt harder than an iron bar and didn't know how much longer he could hold back. When she issued this challenge, he moved so that he was positioned between her legs. Betsy doubled up, her knees almost resting on her chest.

Slocum leaned forward and felt the tip of his manhood brush along the dampness he found. They both shivered lightly. He moved forward even more and sank an inch into a warmth that surrounded him and clung to him fiercely, as if begging for more.

"I need it, Slocum. Don't stop now. Goddamn you, don't stop now!" The woman reached up and gripped his arms. She tugged. He moved forward another inch. The heat boiling from her interior threatened to melt him. He hung on. He wanted more. It had been too long since he'd had a woman. He wanted to make this last as long as possible.

Another inch. And another. Betsy sobbed incoherently. He looked down at her and saw that a rosy flush had risen around her shoulders and neck. When he bent down and kissed her full on the lips, she threw her arms around his neck and pulled him down almost savagely.

He slid into her fully. For a moment, the world froze all around him. No sound, no sight, nothing. The pressure he felt welling up in his balls broke the spell. He pulled back until just the tip of his shaft remained within her, then he rammed forward faster than his initial entry.

Betsy gasped. He repeated the movement, even faster.

"Yes, yes, do it. Go faster, burn me up inside, oh, yes, yes!" Her words slurred as he began swinging his hips in the ages-old rhythm. Betsy began lifting her buttocks off the pallet and ramming forward to greet him. For a moment they remained locked like that, hips grinding in an attempt to plunge even deeper. Then Slocum would withdraw and slip back into her. Friction mounted.

"I . . . I'm so close," she gasped. "Don't stop. So near. So damned near! Aiee!" Betsy's entire body convulsed as she arched her back to take as much of his pounding pillar inside her as she could.

Slocum ground his crotch into hers, but could not withdraw. Betsy had locked her legs around his waist and held him too firmly. He did not try to retreat. He drove forward. A second convulsive shudder passed through the woman.

Like a stick of dynamite he exploded. The tide rose from deep within, then rushed forth uncontrollably. A wash of heat passed through him.

He relaxed and sank forward in the woman's arms. For several minutes they lay together on the thin pallet. When the heat of their lust passed, they both noticed a chill.

"Better get down to work. Jacobson's not paying me to keep you company."

Betsy looked up at him, a smile on her lips. "That's a damn shame!"

5

The Golconda Saloon had turned from an empty room into one filled with shouting miners. The noise stopped Slocum in his tracks. A few minutes earlier he had been with Betsy, earning his reward for rescuing her, and taking advantage of what Jacobson considered "privileges." Slocum doubted Jacobson had meant exactly this, but he wasn't about to tell the saloon owner.

"Hey, Slocum, get down here," shouted Haggerty from behind the bar. The man edged along nervously, one eye on a pair of miners huddled at the far end of the bar.

Slocum wondered what the problem was. Those miners were the quietest ones in the room, and everybody seemed to be enjoying himself. Rowdy, boisterous, crude, maybe even drunk, even though it was hardly sundown, but nobody was doing anything he shouldn't.

He went down the stairs and motioned to Haggerty. "What's wrong?"

Haggerty kept his eyes on the two men. "There's fixin' to be real trouble. Get those bastards outa here!"

Slocum decided asking the barkeep what he saw in the way of trouble brewing would only get him bawled out for not doing his job. Haggerty wasn't his boss, but he had to work with the man. And Slocum might have to convince Haggerty to let him sleep in the back room. Slocum's pockets still lacked two coins to rub together.

Slocum made his way along the bar. The miners saw him and stepped back, some falling silent, others lowering their voices. He couldn't help wondering where the respect came from. Just being the Golconda's bouncer wouldn't cause such reaction. They might have heard how he had knocked out the man who had killed Crapper Jack.

In a small town like Cripple Creek, such gossip traveled fast.

Slocum sidled up to the bar and leaned forward, ears straining to hear what the two men said that had so disturbed Haggerty. Only snatches of the conversation came to him.

A bull-throated roar that silenced the entire saloon brought him around. Slocum reached across and touched the butt of his Colt. It looked as if he'd be needing it damned soon.

Standing in the doorway, his shoulders brushing the sides, was the miner who had been molesting Betsy. The look of fire in his eyes made Slocum wonder if even six .45 slugs would stop this mountain of gristle and pure mean.

"Saints preserve us," one miner gasped. "Tiny is out for blood. Never seen him this riled."

All heads turned toward Slocum. He didn't know if they expected him to keep Tiny out or if they knew who the miner sought with such determination and just wanted to see blood flow.

"You," Tiny bellowed. He pointed at Slocum. "You're the son of a bitch who cold-cocked me!"

"Why don't you go back to the Nugget and finish your drinking there?" asked Slocum. The way the others in the saloon backed away from him made it seem that he had acquired a contagious disease.

Tiny lumbered over and stood looking down at Slocum's six-foot-one height. The man's bad breath might have melted iron. Slocum stood his ground as the miner stared at him.

"Well? You the one?"

"That was no way to treat a lady."

"Hell, you dumb shit, that was Betsy. She's no lady. She's just a two-bit whore."

"I say she is a lady, and you're going to treat her like one."

"You gonna make me?" Tiny demanded. He moved closer, his massive chest bumping against Slocum's.

"Wouldn't want to, unless you force the issue."

Slocum saw the miner's muscles tensing. Flatfooted, Slocum swung, his fist going straight for Tiny's throat. The blow lacked any real power, but it got to its target before the miner's roundhouse started. Tiny gagged, stumbled back, and gasped.

Slocum set his feet, got the range, and unloaded a haymaker that came from somewhere over in Kansas. The powerful blow landed on the side of Tiny's head and knocked him to the floor.

The way Slocum's hand hurt, he knew this was the last punch he was going to land without busting bones. He stepped back, ready to get his Colt into action. It might be murder, since the miner wasn't armed, but Slocum always figured it was better to be alive and arguing the matter than dead and buried.

Tiny sat on the floor, rubbing his face. "Goddamn!" he roared. "No son of a bitch's ever done this to me— twice!"

Then the huge miner laughed. He started laughing so hard that tears ran down his cheeks. "Never thought an itsy-bitsy skinny thing like you'd be able to take me in a fair fight. Son of a bitch. I must be getting old."

"There's only one remedy for that," said Slocum, his eyes never leaving the miner's.

"What's that?" Tiny rolled to his hands and knees and got to his feet. He wobbled.

"You need whiskey. Haggerty, get Tiny a bottle. The

special stuff you keep behind the bar, not that cheap trade whiskey."

Slocum shook his head slightly when Haggerty actually reached for the good bottle. When the barkeep pulled out the whiskey laced with chloral hydrate, Slocum nodded. Haggerty quickly set up the shot and put the bottle down.

Tiny knocked back the shot, then threw the glass over his shoulder. It shattered against the far wall.

"Whatsamatter, little fella? You ain't drinkin' with me?" the voice carried a touch of cruelty with it.

"Hell, if you can't finish one lousy bottle by yourself . . ." Slocum let the words trail off. "Haggerty, get me another bottle. Tiny and I are going to have a drinking contest."

This time Haggerty understood. He passed over another bottle to Slocum, the one reserved for the whores. The amber liquid inside looked like whiskey and carried just enough to smell right, but it was mostly water that had had Mormon Tea boiled in it.

"All right!" cried Tiny. "You ready to go, little fella?"

"Till one of us passes out," promised Slocum. He tilted back the bottle of weak whiskey and began drinking. The brew tasted terrible, but he kept from gagging. The idea of Tiny getting mad was worse. Slocum kept gulping until he saw Tiny start on the laced bottle.

Tiny got half the whiskey down before he began to wobble. Another quarter of the bottle vanished down his gullet before the drug hit him like a mule's kick. Tiny put the bottle down on the bar, belched, and stared at Slocum with eyes that had begun to come unfocused.

"Son of a bitch, you even outdrink me." Tiny fell face forward, stiff as a board. The impact of his massive body hitting the floor shook the Golconda.

"Everybody back to *serious* drinking," Slocum called out. He motioned to Haggerty to help him get Tiny outside.

The pair of them dragged the giant miner outside.

"This is getting to be a habit," Slocum grumbled.

"You're a cool one," said Haggerty, a touch of awe in his voice. "Nobody's ever faced down Tiny like that. What was that he was sayin' about Betsy?"

"Nothing to worry your head over," said Slocum. "How long will he be out?"

"One shot laced with that drug would put a normal man out for twelve solid hours. He drank twenty times that." Haggerty looked at Tiny and shrugged. "He should be back at work with one hell of a hangover tomorrow at sunrise."

Haggerty bent down and rummaged through Tiny's pockets. The barkeep made a wry face and said, "Stone broke. Not even a nickel on him. Must have spent it all at the Nugget, damn him."

Slocum and the barkeep went back into the Golconda. The silence that had fallen when Tiny had entered vanished. Slocum overheard snatches of conversation. Most of it was about him and how he had faced down the meanest miner in the District.

That exaggeration didn't bother Slocum. If anything, it made his job easier. The others were more inclined to give him a wide berth. And the fights he broke up were not the head-breaking, bone-crushing sort.

Slocum made his rounds through the Golconda and positioned himself behind the two miners Haggerty had worried about earlier.

Again Slocum wondered at the barkeep's uneasiness. These two drank quietly, sometimes angrily gesturing at one another, but showing no signs of wanting to have it out. If anything, they seemed to be good friends.

Slocum walked by as one said, "We can do it. Those robbers don't own us!"

"It'll be dangerous. Look." The second one began drawing pictures on the bar, using a finger wet with beer to leave his mark. "We can't move this way or they'll use dynamite on us."

Both stopped talking when Slocum paused. They stared at him, eyes glowing with—what? Slocum thought fervor. Almost a religious fervor. These were men with a cause, and they didn't want to share it with him. He smiled and walked on, aware of them watching until he was out of earshot.

Betsy came down the stairs, waved at him, and smiled. He went to the foot of the stairs.

"Business is good tonight. Getting real polite men, too." Her blue eyes danced. "That wouldn't have nothin' to do with what you did to Tiny, would it?"

"Might," allowed Slocum.

"You're the best thing that's happened in Cripple Creek in a long time," the woman said. She studied the crowd in the saloon and sighed. "So many horny men and so little gold dust on 'em. Wish they'd work harder. It'd make my job a damn sight more lucrative."

"What do you know about the pair at the end of the bar?" he asked Betsy. "Haggerty is really spooked by them."

Betsy frowned. "Just a pair of miners. Don't know their names, but I've seen 'em in here now and again. Nothing much to make me remember who they are. Never been upstairs with me or any of the other girls. Not that I know of, at least."

"Thanks," Slocum said. Haggerty continued to fidget behind the bar as he stared at the two miners. Something bothered the barkeep. Slocum wondered if it was worth his time finding out what.

"Don't worry about Haggerty," Betsy said. "Somebody's always puttin' a burr under his saddle. Jumpiest man I ever saw. Goes with his job, maybe."

"Yeah, maybe," said Slocum. His brief talk with Haggerty about robbing drunk miners didn't show any such nervousness on the man's part. Something about the two miners, something special, got to Haggerty.

A sudden commotion drew Slocum's attention. He turned in time to see one man drunkenly swing at another. Even if the blow had landed, it wouldn't have been dangerous. As it was, the drunk fighter missed by a country mile and fell over a table, spilling drinks and cards.

"Time for me to earn my keep," said Slocum.

"Honey, with me, you can stay for free," Betty said, winking lewdly.

Slocum wished he could take her up on it rather than break up the fight. He decided quickly that it wasn't to anyone's benefit to let them finish inside the Golconda. The pair were too drunk and would only damage property. Slocum ducked under one drunk's punch, grabbed him by the crotch, and lifted. The man gasped. Slocum turned and threw him to the floor. The second drunk started for him, but someone in the crowd smashed a bottle over his head.

"Thanks," Slocum said, not even knowing who he thanked. He grabbed the pair by the collars and dragged them out to the street. The one hit by the bottle stayed out cold. The other Slocum propped up and looked square in the eye.

"You stay the hell out of the Golconda unless you mean to just drink. No fighting. Understand?"

The man moaned and clutched his crotch. He got the message. Slocum heaved a sigh and went to sit in a chair just outside the swinging doors. He'd had enough of the drunks for one night—and it seemed to be just getting roaring.

As he leaned back and stared down Myers Avenue, he heard the two miners inside. They whispered now. This caught Slocum's attention.

"We won't take it no more," the first said. "We got to do something soon."

"This is mighty dangerous. They might fire all our asses."

"Then let 'em," the first one snapped. "We're starving while those robbers are getting rich off our sweat and blood. What we're askin' ain't that extreme. Not when you look at the tons of gold they take from the Independence."

"You got a point," said the second. "Look at old Jake. He busted his damnfool leg and they let him starve."

"Could happen to any of us."

"The others are coming?"

"Any time now."

Even as the miner spoke, Slocum saw a cloud of dust rising from down the street. The tramping of feet would have alerted him if he hadn't been watching. Close to fifty men stopped outside the Golconda, milling around, as if undecided about what to do.

"Evening, gents," Slocum called out. "You got a thirst to quench, this is the place for you. If you're got anything else in mind, I'd suggest you keep on moving."

He stood, his back to the Golconda's door. Those in the street could see nothing but his outline and the way he stood. Slocum had his weight slightly forward, legs bent and his arms hanging at his sides. If any of the miners gave a sign of being trouble, Slocum silently vowed to gun him down where he stood.

He didn't cotton to the notion of losing his life just to keep the peace in Oscar Jacobson's saloon, but he knew the best way of solving problems was to avoid them.

"Who are you?" demanded a miner in the back of the crowd. "We got a right to go in and talk."

"What seems to be your problem?" Slocum asked. "All the problems the Golconda Saloon can solve have to do with having a dry whistle."

Slocum heard the swinging doors behind him but he did not turn. He knew the two miners he had overheard had come out.

"Your friends are getting a mite rowdy," said Slocum. "I don't like that."

"You're nothing but Jacobson's hired gun," snarled a miner. "We ought to string you up."

"Any particular reason, other than you're stupid?" asked Slocum.

The miner started for him. The other held him back. "Wait, Ben. Our fight ain't with him."

"What is your fight? Something wrong at the big mine up on Battle Mountain?" Slocum asked.

"Wages," said the cooler-headed of the two miners. "They ain't payin' us anywhere near what we're worth. We're askin' for three dollars a shift."

"We're lookin' to join the Western Federation of Miners," called out someone in the crowd.

"We got our local a-forming," said the man beside Slocum. "The Free Coinage Union. We done run out all the dagoes, bohunks, and chinks. Now we want to get paid for our work!"

Slocum had no truck with how they eliminated competition, but he had to admit that three dollars a shift wasn't outrageous pay, not from what he heard about the richness of the Independence. "What are you going to do?" he asked.

"We get our raises or we go on strike. And we make damned sure no scabs get brought in to take our places!"

The cheer went up through the crowd. Slocum had held them at bay to this point. He saw that the sentiment had given them courage. Even with a shotgun and a dozen cavalry troopers at his back, he wouldn't tangle with this crowd now.

"Looks like you got a fair claim to me, but what do I know?"

"Where's Jacobson?" shouted the one named Ben. "We got to talk to him."

"What about?"

"Mister, you don't know for nothing, do you? Jacobson owns a majority interest in the Independence Mine. We get him to agree to our wage demands and the others got to follow suit."

Slocum thought on this. He wondered why Jacobson had bothered with Crapper Jack at all. Maybe he didn't like to tend to the day-to-day workings of a business. And why should he when the Independence Mine must be making him a millionaire?

Jacobson's not here," he said. "I don't have any idea where he is, either."

"Burn the place down!" shouted someone in the crowd. "That'll show 'em we mean business!"

Ben started into the Golconda. Slocum grabbed him by the arm and spun him around. "Cool down, now," he said. "I think you got a legitimate grievance, but if you go burning down saloons, there isn't anyone in Cripple Creek who will back you."

"What are we listening to a hired killer for?" Whoever spoke fell silent instantly. They had forgotten why Slocum worked for Jacobson. All through the shouting match, Slocum hadn't backed down an inch or shown the least bit of fear.

"You might listen to common sense," he shouted over the crowd's muttering. "Get four or five of you together. Meet with Jacobson like proper businessmen. If you present it in a way he can approve, you've won."

"We'll swing the bastard at the end of a rope if he don't!"

"Wait," the other miner beside Slocum said, catching Slocum's arm as he reached for his Colt. "We can talk this out—just like you want."

"It's not what I want. I was hired to do a job and I'm doing it. If I let them in, they'll bust up the place."

"Yeah, they will. Might burn it down. They're pretty hot for Jacobson's scalp right now. Can you set up a meeting with him? Just a few of us and him?"

"I don't know. I'm just a hired hand, like they said. I work for a wage, same as you." Slocum looked out over the crowd of miners. He couldn't stand against any pair of them. The fifty would run over him like a buffalo herd.

"I saw the way you handled Tiny and the others. You got the look of a killer, but you don't get any pleasure out of shootin' people down. You use your head."

"Can you control them?" Slocum asked.

"If we can meet with Jacobson, there's a chance."

Slocum studied the miner and decided he could trust the man to try. "I'll do what I can. I have no hold on Jacobson. I only been in Cripple Creek for two days."

"You've already made a reputation, Slocum," said the miner. "I know an honest man when I see him." He turned and yelled, "We got it in the bag, men! Ben and me and Hank and Dirty Bill are gonna meet with Jacobson in the morning."

"Burn the place down to make sure he knows we mean business."

"Save it," yelled the miner. "Save it for tomorrow night—if we don't get any satisfaction on our demands." He looked at Slocum, his face hard. Slocum knew the man meant what he said.

"I'll do what I can," Slocum said.

"Let's get on home, men. We meet here tomorrow night, either to celebrate our raises or to burn the place to the ground."

Slocum sank back into the chair and watched the angry crowd vanish into the night. The wind blowing off Pikes Peak felt even colder than the night before, when he'd slept in Pisgah Graveyard. He wondered if this might not be a forewarning of troubled times ahead. The miners didn't look to be easily sidetracked, and he couldn't imagine Jacobson giving them more than the time of day. He would just have to sit tight and see what happened.

Slocum just hoped he could convince Oscar Jacobson to listen to the miners. If he couldn't, he might be warming his hands at the fire engulfing the Golconda Saloon.

6

Every creak of the Golconda Saloon settling during the night brought Slocum up with his Colt in his hand. Haggerty had not been hard to persuade when Slocum asked him if he could spend the night in the storeroom. After the crowd of miners had left the night before, Haggerty was certain that they would all come back with torches and set fire to the saloon—and to him.

Betsy might have been amenable to letting him spend the night with her over in Poverty Gulch, but Slocum had chosen this colder, less appealing bed for a reason.

He wasn't all that sure that Haggerty was wrong. The miners had been worked up over their wage demands. He had seen a few unions in his day, and they often carried along with their good intentions the worst kind of violence. Men who had been friends turned into bitter enemies. Murders, arson, wanton destruction, all those rode in the saddle along with the union organizers.

Slocum leaned back and strained to hear more of the sound that had brought him awake this time. Nothing. It might have been a cat hunting for its supper. It might have been the cat's supper trying to escape. Whatever the noise was, it didn't come again. Slocum rolled over and put the Colt back on the floor beside his blankets.

Dreams of the gold dust under the Golconda floating across his dreams, Slocum slept until the first light of dawn. He sneezed, pulled the blanket up, and then squinted into the sunrise coming through a small, high window in the storeroom. He stretched and got up. Daylight in the District came late because of the high mountains to the east. He'd have to keep from sleeping the day away if he wanted to find Jacobson.

Slocum prowled through the small kitchen and found some more of the moldy bacon. He fried it and gulped it down with a dipper of water from the well out back. He didn't think he wanted trade whiskey on top of the rancid bacon.

He checked the premises to be sure that he hadn't heard prowlers, ducked under the Golconda's floor and again scanned what would prove to be his personal gold mine, and then went up Myers Avenue looking for Oscar Jacobson. Most of the businesses had opened and some commerce went on already.

He noticed a mixture of attitudes toward him. Some folks were outright friendly. Others ducked inside when he came by. He stopped to talk with one of the friendlier-looking men.

"I'm looking for Jacobson. Have any idea where I can find him this time of day?"

The man got a sour look on his face, then spat. "Jacobson? He's probably still in bed with a whore."

"I get the impression he's not real popular in the District."

The man spat again. "You got that right. Son of a bitch owns most everything in sight, or pieces of it. That don't make him a devil. The way he acts does." The man eyed Slocum, then added, "You got a reputation of being a decent man—for a hired gun. Why don't you hightail it on out of town and leave us be? The mine's no fit matter for you to be involved in for pay."

"All I do is work as bouncer at the saloon. What happens in the gold fields isn't my concern."

"Jacobson hired you to keep peace at the Independence. Everybody knows that. Damned shame that you got a shred of decency in you. Makes hating you harder. Makes killing you 'bout the same, though, when you try to back Jacobson's play."

"Jacobson doesn't pay me enough to die for him. Reckon he doesn't pay the miners enough, either, if three dollars for an eight-hour shift is all they're wanting."

"Them and their damned Free Coinage Union." The man spat, then gnawed off a new bit from the plug of chewing tobacco he had in his pocket. "Don't cotton to the unions any more'n I do the likes of Jacobson. Wish they'd let us be."

"You run the general store?" Slocum indicated Roberts Grocery.

"Do." The man turned and looked up Myers and across to Bennett Avenue. "There's where Jacobson is. At the bank. Him and the lawyer fellow what come in from Denver have been thicker'n thieves of late."

Slocum got the feeling that the owner of the general store meant this literally. Nobody liked lawyers much. One lawyer in a town starved. Two got rich. Slocum didn't want to think on the possibilities when a lawyer and someone like Oscar Jacobson pooled their talents.

Slocum thanked the store owner and hurried on his way. The bank building appealed to him from the standpoint of being easy to rob. He couldn't shake the old habits of scouting a place with the intent to pay it a late-night visit and remove the gold dust in the vaults. But for the clapboard exterior, he saw immediately that the interior vault would not be easily opened.

A heavy steel door kept men like him at bay. Even with a case of dynamite he wasn't sure he could open the vault.

"What the hell do you want?" came Jacobson's querulous voice. "I don't want you nosing around where you don't belong, Slocum. Stay down at the Golconda."

"A word, Mr. Jacobson."

"I heard," the man said glumly. "You want me to talk

with those scalawags from the mine. Those *thieves* from the mine."

"You're not inclined to go along with their wage demands?" Slocum had not thought Jacobson would be willing to give them the pay raise, but he had hoped the man would at least talk with the union leaders.

"Blackmail. That's what it is." A sly look came into Jacobson's eyes. "Besides that, I don't own the Independence outright. I got partners in Denver who have to be notified. That takes time. I can't do this on my own."

"Best to telegraph them in Denver or wherever they might be. That was one whale of an ugly crowd last night."

"You're getting paid well to deal with them. Keep them out of the saloon if they come back."

"They want to burn the Golconda to the ground." Slocum felt a pang at the idea. He needed the saloon intact until he could sift through the dirt under the barroom floor.

"Find some men to help you. Don't pay them more than two dollars a day each."

"I reckon I'll be moving on, Mr. Jacobson. No saloon's worth dying for."

Jacobson's face flushed with anger. He half rose in his chair, then sat back down slowly. The man fought to keep his wrath in check. "You can be replaced, Slocum."

"Just said I quit, unless you talk to the union men. You don't have to agree to give them what they're asking. Just talk."

"That's mighty white of you, not ordering me to give them their blood money." Jacobson took a deep breath. "The Golconda'll be torched unless I talk?"

"Not even God in Heaven can stop them from setting fire to the place if it comes to that. Mr. Jacobson, I talked to them last night. They mean business—and there are a damned sight more of them than you can hire in one day."

"I'll talk to them. You act as messenger, Slocum. But

don't go promising anything more. Just talk."

"That's all anyone wants, Mr. Jacobson." Slocum left, knowing that Jacobson would never agree to the pay demands. But if he talked to the miners, that marked a starting point for both sides. It had to be better than shotguns and torches.

"He'll never agree to giving them a nickel more, John," said Betsy. She and Slocum stood at the end of the bar watching Jacobson and the small knot of miners at a table in the far corner of the Golconda.

"The leader—"

"That's Frank Dennis," Betsy said. "Mighty fine-looking man, ain't he?"

"Dennis looks a mite less than happy at what Jacobson is telling him."

"The son of a bitch will lie enough to keep them calm for a few more days. He might promise them better conditions in the shafts. He might even give them a small raise. But it'll boil over again, mark my words."

Slocum said nothing. He agreed with the woman. Jacobson wasn't the kind of owner to let men earn a decent wage if he could skim money off the top for his own pockets. Deep pockets and short arms was the way his daddy had always described men like that.

He looked around the Golconda. The crowd tonight had never shown. Most of the miners knew of the meeting between Dennis and Jacobson and steered clear. But one man bellied up to the far end of the bar and talked to Haggerty. The barkeep got a disgusted look on his face, then nodded.

"What's going on there?" Slocum asked.

"A down-on-his-luck miner asking for credit, I reckon. Must have some gold dust or Haggerty wouldn't give him the time of day."

"Looks half drunk to start with," Slocum observed.

Betsy shrugged, then went to look over the shoulder of a man in the midst of a low-stakes poker game. She rubbed up against the man winning the most and seductively whispered in his ear. He might have enough to buy her favors.

"No more," Haggerty said in a loud voice. Slocum had come to learn that this was his signal. Haggerty didn't like dealing with the drunks and wanted Slocum to tend to his business as bouncer. "You don't get a damned cent's worth of credit."

"You give it to the others. I know!"

"They pay. What makes you think you could ever pay if you ran up a debt here?"

"I work hard. I . . . I'll be hitting a mother lode any day now. A *real* Golconda!"

"That's what they all say. No money, no whiskey."

The miner wobbled and supported himself against the bar. Slocum knew that the prospector had been drinking in another saloon. Probably the Nugget, since it was only a few yards down the road. The miner had run clean of money, been tossed out, and now came into the Golconda begging for another drink on credit. He had seen it often enough to know that trouble brewed.

"I need a drink. It . . . it's like medicine for me." The man coughed and Slocum thought his lungs would come out. The man was in a bad way with consumption.

Haggerty scowled and turned away. The barkeep yelled when the drunk reached over the bar and grabbed the back of his collar. A surprisingly strong jerk carried Haggerty half over the stained bar.

"Calm down, mister," Slocum said, moving quickly. He grabbed the miner's wrist and squeezed hard enough to make him loosen his grip on Haggerty. The barkeep dropped to his feet, smoothed his wrinkled shirt, and backed off.

"You get him out of here, Slocum. I don't ever want to see him in here again."

"About ready to call it a night, partner?" Slocum asked.

"Don't call me partner. I'm nobody's partner. I work alone. And when I strike it rich, it'll all be mine. Mine and my family's."

"I'm sure it will." Slocum had to grab the miner and hold him up when another coughing fit hit him. "You all right? You sound poorly."

"There's nothing wrong with me," the man snapped. The fire in his pain-wracked eyes told Slocum that the man considered it a weakness to have consumption—and no miner worth his salt admitted to weakness. Not in the District. Not anywhere out West.

As if to make himself out a liar, the miner doubled over and coughed harder than ever. Slocum had seen his share of men with consumption. From the sound of the deadly, rattling cough, this one wouldn't last much longer unless he left the cold, dank, dusty mines and took proper care of himself.

Slocum knew the chances of that happening were about the same as Jacobson giving the miners at the Independence Mine the wages they asked for. The dream of fabulous wealth proved more potent than the fear of death in most gold miners.

"Get him out of here, will you?" Haggerty asked. "He's making a scene. The other patrons don't like hearin' him go on like that. And he's takin' up space others could use."

"Come on, mister," said Slocum, his arm supporting the man. "I'll see that you get home."

"Just one more drink."

"You've reached your limit." Slocum didn't bother to add that the man had run out of money, too. Giving him another drink would cure nothing and might complicate matters.

"I can walk by myself. Don't need your help. Don't need anybody's help." The miner pulled free and stumbled through the swinging doors. Slocum watched him go, wondering if the doors would knock him over. Somehow, he made it without falling over, using his weight to push through. Slocum shook his head. No matter where he traveled, it was always the same. Men who couldn't hold their liquor. Men who thought they knew the odds at poker better than anyone else. Those who sought riches and found only death.

But then, what other way could it be?

The rest of the evening proved quiet. Jacobson, Dennis, and the Battle Mountain miners left, still arguing. Slocum took that to be a good sign. They weren't shooting at each other. How long this "peace" might exist, he didn't want to hazard a guess. Not long, but long enough for him to pick up a few more days' pay before heading on. Cripple Creek had nothing to hold him.

His eyes kept drifting back to Betsy at the top of the stairs. She was a pretty woman and eager to please. But she was nowhere near as pretty as Mina Barclay. Slocum's thoughts kept returning to the proud, lonely woman and how out of place she seemed in the district. He had paid off the remainder of her hotel bill and was still flat busted. That didn't matter too much. He had been there before. He just hoped she had found her husband and settled down somewhere nice along Golden Hill Avenue.

But he doubted it.

"Give me a shot," he told Haggerty. "I need it to keep myself from thinking so much."

Haggerty silently poured. Slocum knocked back the harsh liquor and let it burn all the way down to his belly. The evening was about over. Only a few miners had passed out. Betsy and the others up in the cribs had left. Haggerty made impatient gestures for Slocum to do his job. He went and rousted the drunks and got them moving. They would have a hard time in the company mines or on their own claims tomorrow, but they did this every night. It was a dangerous life and a few hours of drinking gave them their only relief from it.

"That's it," Slocum. "Good night."

"Yeah, good night," mumbled Haggerty as he left. Slocum wondered if the barkeep had it in for him because he hadn't agreed to rob the drunks. Then again, he hadn't come out and said that he wouldn't, either. Haggerty might be hurting for money and was too afraid of the miners to do his own dirty work.

None of this was Slocum's concern. All he needed was a few dollars in his pocket and he could move on. His fists clenched when he remembered the stage holdup. Forty precious dollars lost. And to one of Quantrill's riders. Slocum forced himself to relax. It might be for the best not to tangle with the road agent, no matter how much he wanted his money back. The days of wanton killing were behind him—or so he hoped. Let the man with the scar keep on plundering. That was a matter for the sheriff, not for John Slocum.

Slocum went into the storeroom and spread his blankets. Before he lay down for the night he heard a scraping noise against the wall. His hand flashed to his Colt. On feet as silent as a hunting cougar's, he made his way through the Golconda. The saloon was dark and empty. He went back to the storeroom and pressed his ear against the wall. The noise was louder.

He went to the kitchen and opened the back door. Whirling around, he stood, his weapon cocked and ready. Looking up at him was the miner he had thrown out earlier. The man coughed weakly, then tried to stand. His fingers raked the clapboard wall and made the noise Slocum had heard.

"Why didn't you go on home?" Slocum asked.

"Can't. Too weak to get that far." The man struggled to stand and failed.

Slocum didn't think of himself as a Good Samaritan. But he couldn't have the miner pawing at the walls all night long, especially since he intended to go mining for dust under the saloon for a few hours. Slocum wanted to keep this source of gold dust secret. There would be enough for one, nowhere near enough for two.

"Come on," Slocum said, putting his arm under the other man's and heaving. "We're going to get you home. Where do you hang your hat?"

"Up on Carbonate Hill. A tent. Not much, but it's all I can afford. Until I hit it rich. Until I find the mother lode."

Slocum had heard it before. He slipped his six-shooter into its holster and got the man walking. Once in motion, the miner was able to keep going with only partial support from Slocum.

"Surely do appreciate your kindness. Haggerty would have shot me dead if he'd found me like this."

"Haggerty would have shot his own mother." Slocum didn't even consider what Jacobson would have done. Probably try to work the poor son of a bitch another day in the mine before shooting him.

The man chuckled weakly, then coughed. The man would die before he admitted he had health problems.

"The tent's about a mile up the hill. Sure do appreciate your help. Had one drink too many tonight. A celebration."

"Every night's a celebration," said Slocum.

"No, this was special. Tomorrow I'm going out to stake my claim. Rich one. The mother lode. No one's found it yet. The Independence Mine is rich, but no-where up to what it ought to be." The man leaned more heavily on Slocum as they started up the steep incline of Carbonate Hill. "You could have left me."

"Could have," Slocum allowed.

"I want you to share in my wealth. A small share, but even one part in a hundred will make you a wealthy man. You can buy a fancy house up on Golden Hill. Hell, you can buy the Golconda away from Jacobson, if that's what you want."

"Mostly, I just want to get a good night's sleep," said Slocum.

"Come with me. Help me stake the claim tomorrow morning. It's the least I can do to repay you."

A solitary tent with poorly patched holes in its canvas walls stood on the side of the hill with soft yellow light oozing from under the canvas. Shadows moved against the flapping walls.

"You expecting company?" Slocum asked. "Someone's waiting in the tent."

"My family," said the miner. "You got to meet them."

"Don't think it would be the proper thing to do. Not at this time of night."

"Maybe you're right. But you will come out tomorrow?"

Slocum knew that the miner wouldn't let up until he got a promise. "I'll be back," Slocum said, knowing it was probably a lie.

"Thanks." The man thrust out his hand. Slocum shook it. "You're a good man." Chagrin crossed the miner's face. "Damn, but I forgot to introduce myself. I'm Jonathan Barclay."

Slocum stood and stared. At that instant, the canvas door flap pulled back, and outlined in the dim coal-oil lamp light from inside was Mina Barclay.

7

"Mr. Slocum!" exclaimed Mina Barclay. She stared at him, started to speak again, and then clamped her mouth shut.

"This gent was kind enough to see me home," Jonathan Barclay said. His words still slurred and he fought to keep from coughing out his lungs. Slocum saw the way the miner hunched his shoulders and shook with the effort.

"Mr. Slocum and I have met," Mina said. She brushed back a strand of her brown hair and rocked indecisively from one foot to the other, trying to decide what to do next.

"Glad you found your husband," Slocum said. Thoughts of digging under the Golconda Saloon for gold dust ran through his mind. He might get in an hour or two of work before he got too tired. A week of sifting would be enough for him to leave Cripple Creek in style.

"Please, sir, do come in. You have been very kind to the Barclay family." Mina lowered her eyes and added in a voice almost too soft to hear, *"All* the Barclay family."

"Yeah, come on in and set a spell," Jonathan Barclay

urged. "You can get some of the missus' fine lemonade. She makes it up fresh every day. That's the only way I like it."

"It is a bit on the old side now," Mina said. "I made it this morning." Her expression was so stricken that Slocum knew he couldn't beg off. He had to talk a while. Then he could leave.

And maybe there was more. Mina Barclay was one fine-looking woman. Slocum had to admire her spirit, too. She had stood up well to the road agents and had not broken down when faced with a missing husband when she first arrived in Cripple Creek.

"There's not much room to sit," she said. "Jonathan, find Mr. Slocum a place to sit."

Slocum waited for the man to pull over a three-legged stool. From the rear of the tent came the soft sounds of a sleeping child. Kitty Barclay lay curled in a tight ball, oblivious to everything going on in the tent.

"She can sleep through a war, I do declare," Mina said, a smile replacing the forlorn expression when she mentioned Kitty.

"You two know each other? From Kansas City?" asked Jonathan.

"Mr. Slocum is the gentleman who aided us when we arrived. We owe him ten dollars for the room at the Continental Hotel."

"I'll be goldurned," exclaimed Jonathan Barclay. "Mina had mentioned you, but I never figured you'd be working in the Golconda."

"You took employment at a saloon?" The woman's expression was unreadable now, but the tone of her voice showed her disapproval.

"Pay's good," Slocum said, "even if I don't much like the new owner."

"It must be that Oscar Jacobson. He pert-near owns the entire District."

"There's no way I can dispute that," said Slocum. "I've heard tell of his fingers being in just about every important and rich pie around Cripple Creek."

"I'll buy and sell him when I strike it big," Jonathan Barclay said. His voice grew distant. He lay down on a blanket. His eyelids drooped and his head tipped to his chin. In minutes he slept noisily.

"I apologize for my husband," said Mina. "He was never like this before, when we lived in Utah."

"Gold mining is a hard life, ma'am," said Slocum. He wondered why he was standing up for her husband. The man seemed to be little more than a poverty-stricken beggar, like a hundred others around the District.

"I know. He refuses to return to Kansas City and find real employment."

Slocum held back from asking what the woman thought "real employment" was. Being an eight-to-five clerk in a bank working for men like Jacobson might be as exciting as she could consider. Slocum glanced around the tent with its coal-oil lamp and the dirt floors and decided that kind of life might be right—for her.

A silence fell between them, a silence Slocum found uncomfortable. He broke it, saying, "I'd better be leaving."

The sounds of him standing and pushing back the three-legged stool he had been sitting on woke up Jonathan Barclay. The man peered at him through bleary eyes. "You be back here at sunrise and we'll go stake that claim." The effort of speaking caused Barclay to drop back into a sleep that looked to be more of a coma.

Mina frowned. "Did you agree to go with him?"

"Never came right out and said so," Slocum answered. "I figured anything that would keep him moving in this direction was all right if it wasn't an outright lie."

"It would be nice if someone went with him."

"Consumption?" Slocum asked, knowing the answer. The woman nodded sadly.

Again the heavy silence hung in the air between

them. Slocum said, "I've done my share of mining. A few hours of my day isn't going to mean much one way or the other."

"Oh, Mr. Slocum, it will mean a great deal to him. Thank you." Her brown eyes met his green ones. This time the silence wasn't uncomfortable. She reached out almost shyly and touched his arm. "You've been so good to him—and to Kitty and me. I don't know how to thank you."

"No need." Slocum touched the brim of his hat and said, "I'll be back at sunrise. Can't spend too much time away from the Golconda, though the days are slow."

"I understand. You have work of your own to do. Good night, Mr. Slocum."

"Good night, ma'am."

Slocum slipped into the cold night air and immediately turned up the collar of his jacket to protect his neck. Winter wasn't far away now, from the feel of the wind's icy teeth. Slocum put down his head and walked down the steep slope of Carbonate Hill, regretting his decision to come back in a few hours.

He knew there was only one way to keep his mind off the promise he'd made to Jonathan Barclay. Slocum returned to the Golconda Saloon and got a burlap sack from the storeroom, then dived under the flooring. For two hours he dragged out the loose soil laden with gold dust.

Another hour of panning using water from the well produced almost two ounces of gold. Slocum took another hour to clean up the area to keep others from knowing what he had done.

He fell asleep instantly, the gold dust in a small pouch next to his Colt.

Every muscle in Slocum's body ached as he trudged back up Carbonate Hill. He had worked long hours and hadn't gotten enough sleep—less than three, by his count. Now he had to go traipsing all over the countryside with Barclay, looking for a mythical mother lode.

Some of his weariness vanished when he saw Mina Barclay. The woman had a way about her that set his heart to pounding a little faster. When Kitty pushed through the tent flap and saw him, the smile that broke and crossed her face made the fool's errand worthwhile.

"Mr. Slocum!" the girl cried. "Mama said you wouldn't come, but I knew different."

"I promised, Kitty," he told her. "I always keep my promises. Sometimes it's hard, but I always try."

"I told you so, Mama."

"Yes, dear," Mina Barclay said. The expression she wore was one of amazement. Slocum detected a touch of relief, too. "Would you care for some breakfast, Mr. Slocum? I *am* glad you came. Jonathan needs someone to witness the claim when he files it."

"I thought he was just going out prospecting."

"Oh, no, he has located an area he feels is very rich in sylvanite."

Slocum nodded. The telluride of gold and silver was a sure sign of a workable claim. When the silvery crystals were dropped onto a hot stove, they turned a bright gold. This easy test took the place of an assay, although on a commercial claim Barclay would have to have the expensive tests done.

"Ready to go, Slocum?" Barclay called from inside the tent.

"You both need breakfast first," Mina insisted. She found a battered tin plate and loaded it down with grits. A slice of peach rode alongside. Slocum wolfed it down. It wasn't much, but for the Barclay family it might be the equivalent of a Thanksgiving feast. Nobody lived in a tent unless they had to.

"Finished?" asked Barclay. "I'm rarin' to get out and stake the claim. I swear, Slocum, this is it. This is the one I've been looking for all my life." The excitement flushed Jonathan Barclay's face. He began coughing and tried to hide it.

"Papa, are you all right?" asked Kitty.

"Yes, dear, your father's all right. Be a good girl now

and help me with the plates." Mina hurried her daughter off before she could see how bad this coughing fit was. Barclay spat a gob dark with blood onto the ground.

Slocum stood and waited without saying a word. Barclay controlled his coughing and ducked back into the tent for a moment. Slocum heard the man talking with Mina, but the canvas muffled the words and turned them into a blur.

In a few seconds Barclay ducked back through the canvas door and held up a forked stick. "My dowsing rod," he said. "This will let us know the full extent of the claim."

The men started across the hills and headed west from Cripple Creek. Slocum looked around. "Will we be going far? I don't want to be away from the Golconda too long. Jacobson pays me a good wage." Slocum didn't want to tell Barclay that he didn't want to be fired because of the gold under the saloon. In one night he had taken away more gold dust than Barclay was likely to find in a lifetime with his divining rod.

"Been using this dowsing rod for almost eight years. Done good with it, but this time it gave me a pull so strong that the gold almost yanked the stick out of my hands."

"I've seen men dowse for water but never gold," said Slocum.

"Works the same way. I don't understand how it happens, but I can be walking along, thinking right hard about gold, and all of a sudden the tip of the rod dives down. I know I've got a nugget waiting for me when that happens."

"How many nuggets have you found?" asked Slocum.

"A few. Never very big. Not till now!"

They tramped on across the landscape. Dotted along the hillsides were tailings from other claims. Most had been worked out, or had never amounted to a hill of beans in the first place. Slocum doubted Barclay had found any significant amount of gold this close to Cripple Creek. This would be the first place the miners would look.

They cut down a canyon, went up into the hills, and hiked for almost an hour. When Barclay started looking back over his shoulder to see if they were being trailed, Slocum knew they were getting close to the claim site. Barclay wheezed and coughed and had to sit down. This gave Slocum the chance to study the terrain.

In the distance loomed Battle Mountain with the huge Independence Mine on it. Dust clouds rose from the mine and occasional deep rumblings shook the earth when they dynamited down to new levels. Listening to the miners brag, Slocum guessed that the Independence was about the richest find in forty years—to hear them tell it, even richer than anything found in California in the '49 rush.

He doubted that. What he didn't for an instant doubt was that modern hydro-mining technology had improved the gold yields from a ton of dirt. The ore was pulled out of the ground, crushed, and then blasted with high-pressure hoses. Slocum shook his head. That beat the hell out of panning for gold, but it surely did put a strain on the water available in the District.

"Here," panted Barclay. "This is my claim."

Slocum picked up a rock and looked at it. Throwing it down, he picked up another. "Looks like iron pyrite."

"No, no, it's not all fool's gold," Barclay cried. "That's why nobody's worked this hill. They think it's all worthless. Look!"

He gripped the twin forks of his dowsing rod and began walking around. For a few minutes nothing happened. Slocum grew bored and looked away. From the corner of his eye he saw movement and turned back in time to see the tip of the stick jerking about as if it had a life of its own.

"Here it is! This is the mother lode. I tell you, I'm rich!" Jonathan Barclay walked in ever-widening circles. Slocum followed behind, marking the limits of the claim with tiny cairns of fist-sized rocks. He kept looking toward Battle Mountain and noting how close this hill was to the immense mine cut into its innards. All Slocum had seen on the ground was fool's gold—and a fool waggling a stick around, shouting that he had struck it rich.

"You're my witness," Barclay said. The man sat down heavily on a smooth rock, sweating like a pig. He poked the rod into the ground and wiped his forehead with a soiled bandanna. "You got to sign the deed saying that I staked this out all proper."

Slocum bent down and pulled out a knife. He began digging in the dirt, getting through the sparse vegetation and thin soil, going down deeper for the rock. He scraped the blade along an upjut and pulled the blade out to study it.

"Looks like it might be sylvanite," he said. "Hard to tell without heating it."

"Bring it over here," ordered Barclay. The man coughed, dabbed at his mouth, then reached into a pocket and pulled out a magnifying glass. Slocum held his knife under the lens while Barclay focused. In a few seconds the crystals he had dug up began to sizzle and pop. Then they flowed.

Slocum held it up close and looked hard at the result.

"Looks like gold. Just the right sheen to it. Can't tell without an assay."

"I know all about that," said Barclay. "This might be a vein of sylvanite, and the underlying ore might not be worth digging out. It may assay too low. That doesn't matter. I'll work it and get every speck of gold dust I can."

Slocum understood what the man meant. This might not be the immense commercial find that the Independence had been, but if any gold existed, one man operating it might make an adequate living.

"Why didn't the owners of the Independence Mine simply claim everything in sight?" he asked Barclay. "With a mine that lucrative, you'd think they'd want to be able to follow a rich vein no matter where it ran."

"There's been more'n one man prowling these hills thinking just that, Slocum. Bet none of them ever looked up the records. I did. The syndicate owning the mine failed to lay proper claim to several of these hills around us. Someone's mistake. An oversight. They didn't care. Who can say?"

Slocum stretched his cramped legs and rubbed the gold off the knife blade. It looked and felt right to him, but whether this claim would ever produce gold in any quantity worth mentioning was something he wouldn't have cared to bet on. Yet what Jonathan Barclay said about the company neglecting business made some sense. He had heard of dumber things happening.

When the railroads went through the country getting alternate sections of land on either side of their tracks, they often chose the worst land because no one bothered to do a preliminary survey. They drew lines on maps in Kansas City and St. Louis and San Francisco, and that was that. They made so much money from railroad business they didn't give two hoots in hell about the land.

Slocum believed that long after the iron rails had rusted the land would provide the real wealth.

"You might be on to something big here," he said. "I'd never have given this land a second glance, not being this close to the Independence Mine."

"Let's get on back to Cripple Creek. I want to file this all legal and proper."

"You'll need some samples," said Slocum. "Why not take them back now and save another trip?"

"I got plenty. The divining rod is how I found this claim in the first place. I been out here a couple times and got all the samples I need."

"File the claim, give over the samples for assay," Slocum agreed. They started down the hill and back to town.

"You're cut in for one percent," Barclay said. "That's only fair. Mina told me what you did for her and Kitty when they first got into Cripple Creek."

Slocum wondered if Mina had mentioned that they had ridden the stage together from Colorado Springs. He didn't press the matter. It wasn't any of his business what Mina Barclay told her husband.

Slocum hadn't even worked up a sweat by the time they got to the foot of Carbonate Hill. Barclay was barely able to walk. He puffed and panted and spat a gob of blood every few feet. Slocum was glad that they hadn't brought along any whiskey. Drinking it might have killed Barclay.

"On into town," the man said. He cast a quick look up Carbonate Hill. Slocum knew that the miner wanted to rush up and tell his wife everything. The need to make it legal overrode the desire to boast.

"There's the land office," said Slocum. "I have to get back to the saloon pronto. Let's sign what papers we need to sign and let me get on to work."

"You won't need to work much longer. No, sir," bragged Barclay. "Your cut is going to make you rich. Me, it's going to make me so filthy rich that Leland Stanford will look like a pauper in comparison!"

They went into the small office and waited in line. Half a dozen miners worried their way through claims. Barclay jumped up and down, trying to read over their shoulders to find where the claims were. The men hunched up and made their marks on the paper, wanting no one to see where they hoped to hit it big.

"Got a deed to file," Barclay said when they got to the front of the line.

The bored clerk pushed across the papers. Barclay quickly filled out the form in a bold, flowing script, took a map from the clerk and traced the immediate countryside onto the form, and then drew in a dark box around the spot he claimed.

"That's part of the Battle Mountain claim," the clerk said.

"Look it up. It doesn't belong to anyone. Except me."

The clerk started to order Barclay out, then saw the

way Slocum hitched up his gunbelt. The expression on Slocum's face brooked no delay. The clerk swallowed and went to check. "I'll be goddamned," he said, coming back. "That part of the hill *hasn't* been claimed."

"Show me on the map," said Slocum. The clerk traced out a wedge-shaped portion of the country along an arroyo, running up and across the hill and over to the other side.

"You don't even need to cross Battle Mountain land to get to this spot. If this don't beat all."

"File for the entire section of land," Slocum told Barclay.

"But I don't have enough money for that much. The filing fee goes up with the amount of land."

"Will this cover it?" Slocum asked, dropping his pouch of gold dust onto the counter.

The clerk weighed out the dust in a pan balance, ran a quick test of purity, then used a knife blade to scrape half the dust back into the pouch. "This covers the cost of the filing," the clerk said. "You're damn lucky you could pay for it. I swear, I'd be filing for the land the instant you walked out."

"That's illegal," said Slocum.

The clerk laughed. "Prove it. But there's no need to worry. You got it all filed legal-like."

"Get other witnesses," said Slocum. "Two or three." Barclay hurried outside and convinced two men to return and make their marks on the deed as witnesses.

"Signed, sealed, and all yours, Mr. Barclay," said the clerk. "Don't know how this land escaped being claimed before. No reason except maybe there's nothing on it."

"This is going to be the richest damned claim you ever saw. Wait and see."

"Mention me in your will," said the clerk. He turned to the next miner wanting to file a deed.

"Slocum," said Barclay once they had gotten outside the land office, "you saved me a powerful lot of woe. You rescued Mina and Kitty when they blowed into town when I wasn't expecting them. Now you come through with enough gold dust to let me file for the entire hill. For that I'm going to cut you in for five percent."

"Mighty generous of you." Slocum glanced down Myers Avenue and saw that the early shift from the Independence Mine had started to drift into town. He had to get to work soon. "Why don't you go tell Mrs. Barclay about it?"

"We'll celebrate tonight, Mina and I will. Count on it. And when I get enough out of the mine, I'm going to throw the biggest goldurn bash anyone in Cripple Creek's ever seen. And you're going to be the guest of honor!"

"Can't wait," Slocum said. He watched as Barclay started off for home, walking briskly. The man's gait changed and he began to cough. But he kept on until he turned and vanished from sight.

Slocum went to the Golconda Saloon. Inside he saw half a dozen miners already starting on a long night of drinking.

He stood in the doorway, sizing up the crowd. Before he could step inside, a shot rang and the bullet ripped through his hat and scalp. Slocum fell face forward into the saloon.

8

The saloon spun around in wild circles, the curious faces blurring, the smells vanishing, the floor smashing into Slocum's chest. He bounced and rolled to one side, more from instinct than from conscious thought. He lay on the sawdust-covered floor, stunned.

"Hell's bells!" cried Haggerty. "Somebody went and shot Slocum in the back."

Slocum saw Betsy's concerned face hovering above him, more a fuzzy cloud than distinct features. Her lips moved, but he didn't hear any words. A distinct roar like a freight train started up, grew closer, then engulfed him.

When he awoke he lay on his blanket in the storeroom. Betsy looked down at him and smiled. "You gave us a fright, John. You shouldn't let bushwhackers shoot you down."

Slocum tried to remember everything that had happened. He had left the land office with Barclay, then come to the Golconda. He'd stood in the door for a few seconds to check the crowd. Then had come the hammer blow to the back of his head. He reached up and gingerly touched the bloody groove the bullet had made in his scalp.

"You'll live," Betsy said. "You've got a head harder'n any bullet."

"How long ago did I get shot?"

"About fifteen minutes. Just long enough for the son of a bitch to have hightailed it out of here." Betsy looked down at him and a grim expression crossed her face. "Unless I'm dead wrong, he'd better get on out of Cripple Creek unless he wants to end up dead."

Slocum said nothing. That had been exactly what he was thinking. "Why'd anyone want to backshoot me?" he asked after a while.

Betsy shrugged. "Maybe you riled someone. You're not the most loved person in the District, not working as a bouncer and certainly not working for Oscar Jacobson. Maybe again, it was just a stray bullet that happened to be comin' your way."

Slocum saw that, but something else bothered him. "The only ones I've had any real run-ins with are Tiny and the one who killed Crapper Jack."

"McKinnie. He's a low-life. Yeah," Betsy said, "he's coward enough to gun a man down when his back's turned. But what would be in it for him? Jacobson's already let him off scot free for killing Jack. He'd be looking to keep a low profile, not to make new trouble."

Slocum sat up. The dizziness passed and he came to his feet. It took several seconds and Betsy's willing arm around his waist before he could walk.

"You don't have to go back out there. Not yet, anyway," Betsy said. "You should rest up a while."

"Jacobson's not paying me to sit around."

"There's something else, isn't there?" Betsy asked.

"I don't want whoever shot me thinking he can get away with it. If I keep my hat pulled down, the wound won't show. Let him believe he's a lousy shot—or I'm made out of smoke."

Betsy shook her head and started him toward the door leading into the main saloon. The noise hit Slocum like a blow. He reeled and recovered before he reached the end of the bar. To Haggerty he said,

"Give me a shot to steady my nerves."

The barkeep looked pale and drawn, as if he had been the one shot. "You must be made out of steel," was all he said as he shoved across a shot glass of cheap whiskey. Slocum knocked it back and let the liquor give him strength.

He rested against the bar as he studied the men in the room. Two tables had faro games going. Half a dozen miners gathered around another table where a gambler dealt Spanish monte and robbed them blind. Most simply drank—alone, in pairs or groups—but they all drank heavily. Slocum wondered if the real gold mine in Cripple Creek wasn't within these four walls.

A miner fumbled with his poke and measured out gold dust none too carefully. Slocum smiled as dust sparkled in the air and settled to the floor. Boots moving over the spilled dust carried some off in mud. Other grains fell between the cracks and into the muck below. A few more "mining" expeditions beneath the Golconda would give Slocum a stash worthy of the name.

An hour passed. Slocum had begun to relax and think that the trouble for the night had passed. The shot that had struck him might have been a random bullet fired for no reason. Drunk miners celebrated by firing into the air all the time. He might have just been unlucky and in the wrong place at the wrong time.

But as much as Slocum wanted to believe this, he couldn't. His gut feelings told him that someone had tried to murder him. Of all the people he knew in Cripple Creek, the most likely one had to be McKinnie. But why?

He had just begun to worry over the problem when a round of shots crashed through the thin walls and the glass window. Shattered fragments from the window blasted through the Golconda and cut several miners playing faro. The heavy bullets did little real damage, their power spent penetrating the saloon's thin clapboard walls.

Slocum had his Colt out and was headed for the door

before the first cry of outrage rose from a miner's throat. He spun through the Golconda's swinging doors and went into a crouch, the cocked weapon swinging left and right, ready for action.

His head almost exploded from pain, but the sight of men in the street really shook him. He thought he had returned to the War and had got himself caught up in a skirmish. Slocum dropped to the street and ducked under the boardwalk, a hail of buckshot ripping away the spot where he had stood.

Slocum started to return fire, then held back. The crowd looked nasty. The union miners carried torches and most had shotguns or rifles. To shoot into the crowd would be to kill someone, maybe several people. What held Slocum back was the notion of shooting and having the mob rip him apart. Too much firepower could be directed against him should he choose to run. He sank down into the muck under the boardwalk and waited.

At the front of the crowd stood Frank Dennis. The expression on the man's face told Slocum that there would be no reasoning with any of the miners. They sought blood, and nothing less would satisfy them.

"Get that son of a bitch Jacobson out here!" someone at the rear of the mob shouted. "I want to string him up!"

A dozen men thundered into the Golconda. Slocum ducked instinctively as they tramped above his head. He wriggled through the cold mud and got out at the side. He circled the building—and was glad that he had. At the rear of the Golconda two miners knelt. One held a torch and the other worked to pile kindling against the wall.

Slocum cocked his Colt and aimed at the man holding the torch. "Keep your hands in sight and don't drop the torch," he ordered in a cold voice.

The one working on the wood spun, fell to his knees, and reached for the pistol thrust into the waistband of his trousers. Slocum's Colt barked loud and sharp. The man jerked upright and fell face down in the dirt.

"You can join him or you can leave. Nobody's setting fire to the saloon." Slocum pointed the Colt directly at the shaking man's face, letting him look down the huge bore.

"'We didn't mean nothing by this. We want Jacobson."

"Then find Jacobson. Any damned fool ought to know that a fire in Cripple Creek would spread faster than a whore's disease. You burn down the Golconda and you might burn down the whole town."

"You didn't have to kill Max."

"He didn't have to reach for his six-shooter." The unwavering aim Slocum held on the miner totally unnerved the man. He turned and ran like all the demons of hell chased him.

Slocum considered a bullet to the back of the man's head. Any coward who would burn down a saloon full of people didn't deserve to live. He released the hammer and lowered it. Slocum put out the torch and dragged Max's body away from the back door. If the new sheriff ever arrived from Denver, let him find the body somewhere else than at the Golconda's rear door.

Slocum went in the back way, edged through the storeroom and into the saloon proper. Haggerty lay on his back, an ugly cut on his head bleeding enough to let Slocum know that the barkeep was still alive. What caught his full attention was a pair of men dragging Betsy between them. They passed through the swinging doors and went outside.

The crowd roared approval.

"Hang the whore!" came the shout.

Slocum hastily snapped open the cylinder of his Colt and replaced the spent round, then bent down and pulled a Colt Navy from Haggerty's hand and thrust it into his belt. Without another thought, he plunged through the doors and came out behind the two men holding Betsy.

Slocum swung his Colt as hard as he could and caught the man on the left behind the ear. The stocky miner never made a sound as he dropped. Betsy yelled and jerked free of the other man. Slocum kicked him in the crotch and stepped back, his gun cocked and aimed at the mob.

"Frank Dennis," he called out. "What's going on here?"

"You, you're Slocum, ain't you?" Dennis moved closer and held up a sputtering torch that illuminated Slocum's face. "We've got no quarrel with you. You played fair with us before. We want Jacobson."

"Then find him. He's not here."

"Hang'em both!" an agitator in the crowd demanded. "Stretch their damned scrawny necks. That'll show Jacobson the power of the Free Coinage Union!"

The surge of the crowd caused Slocum to fire over their heads. At the sudden report the men in front stopped. Those behind ran into them; many went down in a tangle of flailing arms and legs.

"Dennis, I've got no quarrel with you. I think you deserve the wages you're asking."

"That son of a bitch *cut* our pay!" Dennis exclaimed. "We only want what's fair. A dollar fifty a shift ain't it!"

"Take another step forward and you're buzzard meat," Slocum said. He aimed the Colt at Dennis's face as he slipped Haggerty's six-shooter from his belt and held it loosely in his left hand.

A miner at the edge of the crowd dashed forward and grabbed Betsy. Slocum lifted the Colt Navy and fired twice. Neither bullet hit the man, but both came near enough to convince him to think twice about rushing onto the boardwalk.

"You're the one who's gonna be buzzard meat, Slocum. Look in front of you, man! You're outnumbered fifty to one!"

"A few of you will be dead if you try torching the saloon again," Slocum said. "I'm not being paid enough to die for Jacobson or even keep the Golconda from going up in flames, but this is the only way I can see myself getting clear of this alive."

"You'll die if you don't just walk away now," said

Dennis. Slocum saw sweat beading on the miner's forehead in spite of the cold wind whipping down Myers
Avenue.

"Looks like I might be dead either way. Since that
seems to be the case, some of you will go with me."

For several seconds a hush fell over the crowd. Only
the noise of the wind and the crackling of the tar torches
could be heard. Then Slocum saw motion in the crowd.
A path parted for Tiny. The huge miner lumbered up.
Standing two steps down from the boardwalk, he still
looked Slocum square in the eye.

"Get 'im, Tiny. Make 'em pay!"

"Shut up," the giant yelled. "Slocum's all right. Any
man what kin drink me under the table is my friend."
Tiny turned and faced the crowd. "What you do to him,
you got to *try* and do to me first."

A nervous whisper rose from the crowd.

"Slocum beat the stuffing out of me. Any man who
can do that *and* drink me under the table's my good
friend." Tiny turned and looked at Slocum, then almost
shyly tipped his hat in Betsy's direction. "Evening,
ma'am," he said.

If Slocum had not been facing fifty men intent on a
necktie party, he'd have laughed at the giant miner's
civility toward Betsy.

Two others moved forward. "Tiny, you got the
strength of a mule—and the manners, too. But we're
not going to fight you." They shifted from foot to foot,
then edged off in the direction of the Nugget Saloon.

Slocum saw others in the crowd begin to slip away.

"Dennis, let's talk this out." Slocum didn't want to
embarrass the man in front of his union members. To
have done so would have created an implacable enemy.
Slocum thought Dennis was an honest man caught up in
matters he didn't know how to control.

"You bet we're gonna talk, Slocum," Dennis called
out loudly. "The rest of you men get on home. Let me
work this out."

That got Dennis off the hook. Slocum slipped his

Colt back into his holster. Betsy and Tiny entered the Golconda first. Slocum followed, a prickly feeling up and down his spine as he wondered if Dennis might try to backshoot him. If he had judged wrongly, Dennis would kill him. If not, there might be a chance to smooth over the dispute.

Slocum stepped over Haggerty's unconscious form, dropped the barkeep's Colt onto his belly, and went behind the bar. He found a bottle of whiskey and brought it back. He pointed to a table in the back. He and Frank Dennis sat down facing one another across the stained tabletop.

Slocum poured a shot for Dennis, then one for himself. He raised his glass in silent toast, then drank. He refilled both glasses before saying, "I just got into Cripple Creek, so I'm not entitled to an opinion."

"But you got one anyway," said Dennis. "And you're gonna make me listen to it."

"You're not going to move Jacobson with a mob. That's the kind of action he expects. How long would it take him to bring in union busters from Denver?"

"A week."

"You can bet that they're on the way right now. No, wait," Slocum said, holding up his hand. Dennis sank back into the hard chair, eyes blazing. "I don't know anything about Jacobson's business dealings, but think on it. If you were the owner of a big chunk of the Independence and wanted to make even more off it, how would *you* go about protecting it?"

"You got a point. This just means we've got to arm everybody in the union."

"There's that," said Slocum. "You can do something else, too. You might do something he's not expecting."

"What?" Dennis looked suspicious.

"Talk with him. Maybe compromise. Convince him that he's in for a world of trouble—and expense—if he doesn't go along with a wage increase."

"We want three dollars for an eight-hour shift!"

"You deserve it," Slocum said. He heaved a deep

sigh. He should let Jacobson do his own dirty work. All Slocum wanted was to keep the Golconda standing and in business long enough to work through the silt underneath the floorboards. A dozen ounces of gold would do him nicely. He reckoned that might mean a week's work.

He wasn't likely to get a better opportunity to make a dime in Cripple Creek or anywhere else.

"We could blow up the mine. We can put dynamite in the stoops. It'd take a year to dig back down to the gold."

"Let him know this, subtle-like. Don't make him bristle like a boar-hog. That'll only make everyone wish it hadn't happened."

"What do you get out of all this?"

Slocum wasn't about to tell Dennis. "Let's say I've seen my share of trouble. All I want is some peace and quiet."

"Bullshit." Frank Dennis worked on the whiskey. Slocum refilled his glass. Dennis worked over all that Slocum had said and finally came to a conclusion. "The union's got to get some concessions from Jacobson and the other owners soon. Otherwise, there will be trouble."

"Seems as if that's up to you," Slocum said mildly.

"You're not involved with any of Jacobson's other schemes, are you? You got the look of a killer about you, but you sure as hell don't act like it." Dennis finished the whiskey. "Nobody's made friends with Tiny this fast in a long time."

"He's hard to get to know," said Slocum, smiling. "But he's got a touch of good in him."

"Yeah, and you brought out the touch by beating him senseless. That's the only way."

"Whatever works."

"That's odd advice, Slocum. Whatever works. I ain't sayin' you're not mixed up in Jacobson's crooked schemes, but I am sayin' that you seem like a decent enough fellow."

"A last drink before you go?" Slocum held up the almost empty bottle.

"Since we're not paying for it, we might as well." Dennis and Slocum toasted each other silently. The miner wiped his lips on his sleeve and left, stepping over Haggerty as he went. The barkeep stirred and sat up, holding his head.

His six-shooter dropped to the floor. He grabbed for it, fumbling around until he got his finger on the trigger.

"There's no one around to shoot, Haggerty. You might as well put that away." Slocum drained the bottle and set it on the table.

"The miners. They wanted to lynch me. One hit me."

"It's all done with for tonight." Slocum doubted that Jacobson would agree to any terms come up with by the union, but the Golconda's owner might hold off trouble for a week or more.

"The place is empty," Haggerty protested. He got to his feet, using the bar to support himself.

"Have a drink, then close up," said Slocum. "There's not going to be any more customers in here tonight."

"But the cribs?" Haggerty turned and looked up at the stairs.

"Just Betsy up there," said Slocum.

The sounds echoing down the stairs told Slocum what the woman and Tiny were doing.

"She's got a customer."

"Haggerty, close the damned saloon for the night. Betsy doesn't have a customer."

"But . . ." Haggerty touched his head and his fingers came away bloody. This convinced him that he might not understand what was happening, and that it no longer mattered to him. He tucked the pistol away and took the money from the till. Still shaking his head, Haggerty stumbled out into the night.

Slocum listened to Betsy's and Tiny's passionate sounds and wondered if they might not do what the crowd had failed to do—bring the Golconda's walls crashing down. He smiled and went into the back room.

It had been a busy day. With any luck, he'd have an extra hour's worth of digging around under the flooring tonight. That might make facing down the crowd of miners worthwhile.

Slocum doubted it. But the gold would still be mighty soothing.

9

Slocum awoke to the sounds of lovemaking. He looked around the storeroom, his sleep-dazed mind thinking he was somewhere else. He rolled to a sitting position and listened hard, then laughed. Tiny and Betsy had not left the night before and were still upstairs. It amazed him what getting some politeness beat into a thick head might do. Slocum had seen that Betsy liked Tiny, but not his crude ways.

That had apparently changed for the better.

He lay back, stretching. His hand reached out to touch the bag of gold dust he had recovered from under the saloon. It was almost as much as the first night's work. If he kept this up for a solid week, he might recover as much as a pound of gold dust. He did the figuring in his head and came up with the sum of three hundred dollars. That, with the wages from Oscar Jacobson, made his stay in Cripple Creek worthwhile.

He got up and put his blankets in the corner of the storeroom, then stashed the pouch of gold dust where no one would find it. Haggerty spent as little time back here as possible, not liking the idea of being alone. Slocum guessed the man had a bad conscience from all the miners he had drugged and Crapper Jack had robbed.

Haggerty might figure that one of the miners might piece it all together and come after him.

Slocum scratched his head as he thought about Haggerty. A strange man in many ways. He wondered what secrets the barkeep had overheard—and used to his benefit. Many, Slocum thought. Haggerty was the kind of man who always looked for the easy way, the angle, the way of getting around doing an honest day's work.

At this Slocum had to laugh. Who was it sifting through the muck beneath the Golconda looking for lost gold dust? If that wasn't a way of avoiding an honest job, he didn't know what was.

Slocum left the saloon, the soft moans Betsy made echoing after him. He hitched his gunbelt up and studied the muddy, rutted path that was Myers Avenue. It looked like a different world from last night. Gone were the miners with their torches and shotguns. Only an occasional buckboard and team appeared. A few men and women walked about, intent on the first doings of a new day. Slocum strolled the streets, his feet taking him toward Carbonate Hill.

He stopped at the base of the long climb, wondering if he should go up to the Barclays' tent. He felt an obligation to Mina Barclay that he shouldn't have. It was no one's fault that she had come to this godforsaken town following her husband, unless blame could be placed on Jonathan Barclay. Slocum wasn't about to do that.

For all the man's consumptive cough, he had the dream. What was a man without the dream that gave life meaning? For some it was power. For Barclay it was wealth. Slocum stared up the hill and wondered what his was. It wasn't power. He had tasted some of that in the War. As a captain he had commanded men. As a sniper he had the power of life and death resting at the tip of his finger. When he'd ridden with Quantrill, he had felt the power they had over the populace every time they rode out. It wasn't power.

Nor was it money. He didn't mind the feel of a hefty poke of gold dust swinging at his belt. A wad of greenbacks big enough to choke a cow wasn't anything he would turn his back on, either. But would he ever descend as far as Oscar Jacobson in the quest for wealth? Slocum doubted it. Jacobson got rich off the sweat of the miners' brows. That wasn't to Slocum's liking.

What did he want? Slocum frowned when he couldn't come up with a good answer. To see what lay beyond the sunrise, to hunt in a land filled with beauty, to be free. *Hozro*, the Navajos called it—walking in beauty. Those he wanted—those he had. What was his dream?

"Mr. Slocum!" came a shrill cry. "You've come by to see me!"

"Hello, Kitty," he said. "Actually, I was just passing by and stopped for a rest."

The girl smiled shyly. "Are you coming up to see Mama? Papa's already off at the claim getting rich."

"Kitty," he said slowly, trying to decide if he ought to say anything to her about her father. "The claim looks good. Your pa's a lucky man to get it like he did, but there's no guarantee that there's spit on that hill."

"Papa says there's gold, that you saw the way the divining rod almost pulled out of his hands when he crossed the mother lode." The girl's solemn recitation and complete trust of her father's skills as a prospector couldn't be argued with.

"Let's see if your ma's got any of that fresh-made lemonade done yet. It's getting on to winter, but it's still mighty hot and dusty."

"Mr. Slocum," Kitty said, her big eyes looking up at him, "there's something I want to confess."

"What's that? You haven't got into any trouble, have you?"

"The lemonade isn't fresh. Mama makes it from all manner of things. It tastes close to fresh, but it isn't."

Slocum laughed. "That makes no nevermind with me. If anything, your mother's inventiveness makes it taste even better." He followed Kitty up the hill to the tent.

"Kitty," called Mina Barclay. She poked her head out of the canvas flap, saw Slocum, and smiled broadly. "Mr. Slocum, I thought it was just Kitty."

"Good morning, ma'am," he said.

Mina started to say something, stopped, then said, "Again I am in your debt for what you did for Jonathan yesterday. It's been ever so long since I have seen him that thrilled about anything. I do believe this has been good for him."

"I've seen men dowse for water but never gold," Slocum said. "There's a heap of work ahead for him."

"I'm sure there is, Mr. Slocum...John." Her soft brown eyes hesitantly found his green ones.

"He'll do all right, Mina."

Mina Barclay looked away quickly, as if she had done something she wasn't proud of. "There's not much I can offer you. The larder's bare. I need to go to Roberts Grocery and get some provisions."

"Not a bad idea," Slocum said. "The day's mighty warm now, but winter comes quick in the Rockies. But then, you know that, since you lived over in Utah."

Mina looked down the hill. "I don't cotton much to the notion of being trapped up here when the snows come." She shrugged in resignation. "Not much to do, since this is the best we can do until Jonathan proves the claim."

"There's advantages to being up here. You missed the ruckus in town last night." Slocum went on to tell her about the Free Coinage Union and the trouble at the Golconda.

"You're very brave, Mr. Slocum," said Kitty, her eyes wide.

"Brave?" Slocum shook his head. "I didn't have any choice. That's not bravery. If I'd run they would've cut me down. So I had to stay. That was the only chance I had."

"You stood up for that wh—" Mina bit off the word. "You stood up for that woman. Seems to me that you're doing that a considerable bit these days."

Again they looked at one another. The thought came and went through Slocum's mind that this might be his dream, what he had sought for so long. Mina Barclay was a lovely woman, intelligent, capable, and with a level head.

From outside came a loud cry. Seconds later, Jonathan Barclay pushed back the tent flap and stumbled into the tent. "I done it, Mina! I done it this time, just like I said I would! Look at this. Just look!"

He thrust out a chunk of ore in her direction. The woman took it gingerly, turning it over and over. Slowly her expression changed from distaste to an excitement matching her husband's.

"Mr. Slocum," she said. He noticed that in her husband's presence she had turned formal once again. "What do you make of this?"

Slocum's experienced eye caught the gold flecks instantly. He went to the tent flap and examined the ore in the sunlight. He pulled out his knife and ran the tip through the vein, then looked at it closely.

"Not pyrite," he said. "Don't know of any minerals that look like this except fool's gold . . . and real gold."

"There're tons of this ore under that hill. And it's mine. Mine, all mine!" Jonathan Barclay grabbed Mina and began swinging her around. "Darlin', we're rich!"

Barclay settled down, then broke into a fit of coughing. Slocum studied the ore and had to admit that it looked good. If the ore existed in commercial quantities, Barclay might have a claim as rich as the Independence Mine.

"I need to get it assayed," he said, the coughing fit passing. He spat a dark black gob onto the ground just outside the tent. Slocum noticed the caked mud there; Barclay had done this more than once recently. "Only trouble is, we don't have the money for it."

"Won't cost that much," said Slocum. He looked from Barclay to Mina to Kitty. "I staked you for the filing fees. I can stake you for this."

"I gave Slocum five percent of the claim, Mina,"

Barclay said. A note in his voice made Slocum stiffen. Now that he had hit it big, Barclay was regretting his earlier generosity.

"You can keep the five percent," Slocum said, "and just repay me what I spent."

"Please, John," Mina spoke up. "If Jonathan promised a share, you deserve it."

"Does this mean I can get my silver dollars back, Mama?" Kitty asked. She turned to Slocum and said, "I had to use them to buy food. We were getting very hungry."

"You'll get them back and a thousand more!" promised Barclay. "Come on, Slocum, let's get the ore assayed. I know it's going to be rich. Maybe richer than over on Battle Mountain. Damn, but this is a good feeling!"

Together Slocum and Barclay went into the land deed and assay office. The same clerk who had taken the claim the day before looked up, surprised. "You wantin' to sell off your deed so soon?" he asked.

"I want this assayed right now." Barclay shoved the ore sample across the counter. The clerk made a face, then looked at Slocum, who stood with his hand resting on the butt of his Colt.

"Heard you had some trouble at the Golconda last night," said the clerk. "Something about you facing down a mob of liquored-up miners bent on hellraising."

"Rumors get bigger every time they're told," said Slocum.

The clerk pulled out chemicals from under the counter. The bottle with the glass stopper carried a label proclaiming the contents to be aqua regia. Slocum watched as the clerk used a dropper to transfer a bit of the acid to the ore. All three crowded closer as they watched the potent acid attack the ore.

"Can't tell you much about the purity," said the clerk, "except it ain't nowhere near as good as over at Battle Mountain."

"But it is gold?" demanded Barclay.

"The aqua regia dissolved this." The clerk held out a white cloth with a gold smear on it. "I take it to be gold. You got yourself a good claim, Mr. Barclay."

Jonathan Barclay almost collapsed, laughing, crying, coughing, and shouting out in triumph. "This calls for a drink. It's on me, Slocum!"

"What's this hunk of ore worth?" Slocum asked, cutting off the jubilant man's celebration.

"I'll take a chance on it and give you five dollars. Don't think there's a quarter-ounce in it, but there might be." The clerk's eyes gleamed. Slocum knew the man had already estimated the value and made a profit on the deal. But five dollars for a piece of unworked ore was a fine reward for a single day's mining.

"Give it to him," said Slocum. To Barclay he said, "Now you can buy me the drink. Haggerty doesn't give the hired help free drinks—and Oscar Jacobson wouldn't be pleased if he tried."

Together they went to the Golconda. Barclay used the money he'd just received to buy a bottle. Slocum put his hand on Barclay's wrist. "You got a wife and child up on Carbonate Hill with gnawing pains in their bellies from hunger. Why not spend the money on food?"

"This is a celebration, Slocum. Here, drink up."

Slocum took one drink and refused a second. Barclay had already poured a third down his gullet but Slocum got fed up with the man and left the saloon. It was one thing to be happy about a major find. It was something else again to forget a loving wife and child.

Slocum wandered Cripple Creek's streets aimlessly. It was almost sundown when he stopped and saw that he had returned to the foot of Carbonate Hill. He looked up and saw the coal-oil lantern shining wanly inside the tent. From the shapes outlined on the canvas, he didn't think Jonathan Barclay had returned from his celebrating yet.

Slocum started to go up the hill, then stopped. It was time to go to work. He made sure his Colt rode easy in his holster and headed back to the Golconda.

It didn't surprise him one whit to find Jonathan Barclay drunker than a skunk, and still celebrating.

10

Slocum watched the last of the customers drag out of the Golconda Saloon. They had been rowdy tonight and he was tired of the bickering, the fights, and the sudden flare-up of tempers that had left one man with a minor gunshot wound in his ass.

Slocum shook his head. If the man facing him down had been a better shot, or less drunk, it might have been serious. As it was, everyone had found it funny, even the man who'd been shot. When the liquor wore off, he'd be in a world of hurt. Until then, everyone had gone back to being friends.

Looking over his shoulder, he saw Tiny and Betsy at a table in the corner. They were billing and cooing like a pair of turtledoves.

"You two are going to have to get out of here. I'm tired and I want to see the place shut up."

"What's wrong with Haggerty? He usually does it."

"Haggerty left like his coattails were on fire," said Slocum. He went over and sat in the chair opposite Betsy. Tiny had a huge arm around her shoulders and she snuggled down into the man's shoulder. "Told me to close up and that was that."

"Slocum," said Tiny, "I want to ast you somethin'."

The huge miner's tone put Slocum on his guard. "What is it?"

"Me and Betsy, well, we been thinkin' about gettin' hitched."

If Tiny had hit Slocum with one of his meaty fists, he couldn't have been more stunned.

"And I was wonderin' if you'd stand up and be my best man. I know this seems sudden-like and all, but there's a travelin' judge comin' through town next week."

"We might not get a better chance for some time," said Betsy. "And I was brought up believing that a man and a woman living together ought to be married."

"Congratulations," said Slocum. "I'd be happy to stand up with you."

"Thanks. And we're gonna throw one hell of a party. I saved up some of my wages from the mine. It ought to be enough to have a couple dozen friends whoopin' it up."

Slocum's mind worked quickly through the numbers. If he got under the Golconda and found another couple ounces of gold dust tonight, he might have enough by the time Tiny and Betsy got married to get himself a horse and ride on out. Their wedding gave him a target to shoot for. He couldn't see himself staying around the Cripple Creek District much longer than that.

Even if he was part owner of Jonathan Barclay's mine, he had to be moving on. Slocum turned bitter when he thought on Barclay. The man had gotten falling down drunk and two miners from the Independence Mine had to carry him out. Slocum refused to nurse-maid the man any more. The idea of leaving Mina and Kitty alone on the top of the hill was bad enough, but squandering the money on whiskey when they needed food turned Slocum cold inside.

But that wasn't any of his concern. He kept telling himself this and he knew he kept lying when he did.

It was a damned shame that Barclay treated Mina the way he did.

"We're fixin' to leave, Slocum," said Tiny. "We got better things to do than stay here jawin' with you all night."

"Reckon you do," he said, smiling at them. Slocum rose and pushed the chair back. Then he froze. Something wasn't right. He turned slowly, then went cold inside. Reflected in the mirror behind the bar were dancing flames.

"Fire!" he shouted. "The whole damned town's on fire!"

Slocum rushed to the swinging doors, thinking that one of the drunk union miners had returned and made good on the threat to set fire to the saloon. But the blaze came from down Myers Avenue and ran in a fiery line out of sight down Bennett. Even as he realized that the flames were twice as tall as any of the buildings in Cripple Creek, the fire bell began its mournful tolling.

"This looks like a bad one," said Tiny. "I seen one, two fires before, but they wasn't nothin' compared to the look of this one." He quickly kissed Betsy and took off at a lumbering run.

Slocum followed on the giant's heels. They turned the corner onto Bennett at the same time and pulled up short. Six stores had already burned to the ground. Sparks flew from the blaze and landed on the roof of Roberts Grocery and the nearby land office.

"Lend a hand, you two," called a man with a bandanna wrapped around his upper arm.

"Anybody who's got a bandanna on like that is a fire marshal," said Tiny. "Do what they say or get yourself shot." The giant miner hurried to a pump handle and began turning the crank, doing the work of two men. Slocum joined him. Between them they kept the pump drawing water from the creek a quarter of a mile away.

The water poured from the house and into a long trough. Men formed a bucket brigade and tossed the water onto the raging fire.

"They might as well be pissin' on it, for all the good they're doin'," said Tiny.

"The fire will burn itself out eventually," said Slocum. He hoped that they could stop the blaze here. If it worked its way back around to the Golconda Saloon, he was out any chance of finishing his nocturnal mining.

"There goes the damn grocery store," said Tiny, ducking as sparks flew into the air from the collapsing roof.

Slocum watched helplessly as the land office followed. The building beyond that—he thought it was the funeral parlor—burned quickly and left only a jumble of charred wall studs. All the while the fire burned, Slocum kept working on the pump.

His shoulders began to ache and he gasped for air. The wound he had gotten the night before caused his head to feel like a rotted melon ready to burst. But he kept working. The hungry fire dined vigorously. If he flagged now, the blaze would consume all Cripple Creek.

Slocum started to slow down in his efforts to keep the pump turning and the water flowing. Only the sight of the huge man across from him kept Slocum going. Tiny refused to stop. Sweat beaded his forehead and the droplets reflected the dancing flames. The combination turned him into something more than human.

"Keep goin', little fella," Tiny panted out. "We'll lick it. Just you wait and see."

"Does the town catch fire often?"

"Too damn often for my taste. The buildings are all like kindling. Never seen a place this bad. Summer's been dry, too. Rains come and turn the streets to mud, then it dries off by noon the next day. Hell of a way to live."

Slocum had spent the entire time in Cripple Creek sloshing around in mud, watching it dry out to a dust, then turn to mud again in the next brief downpour. And under the Golconda Saloon he'd crawled around in muck. It was hard for him to believe that the season had been dry.

Even though he hurt all over, Slocum kept up the

work. The fire slowly retreated in the face of so much
water being dumped on it, but the buildings were completely ruined.

"How much longer?" Slocum asked. "Is anyone
going to spell us?"

"Everyone else is on the bucket line." Tiny bent his
back to the work and kept the pump turning, giving
Slocum a chance to ease off a mite.

Slocum's hands fell off the pump handle and he
stepped away.

"Hey, Slocum, get your ass back here. I'm not doin'
all the work. I was just giving you a rest."

"There's someone in that building. What is it?"

"Was the National Hotel. What do you mean, someone's in there?" Tiny squinted into the bright flames
chewing away at the ground floor of the hotel. Most of
the exterior had been blackened and the signs had fallen
off. Inside rose a solid wall of flames.

"Second story. At the rear. See?" Slocum was already on the way across the street and down the alley
beside the ravaged hotel. The heat boiling from the fire
blistered his hands and face. He whipped off his bandanna, dipped it in the trough, and tied it over his face.
This kept out some of the smoke, but most of all held
back the intense heat clawing at his flesh.

"Slocum!" bellowed Tiny. "The water's more important!"

Slocum came to the side door. He never looked back
at the giant miner. He knew what Tiny said was true,
but others could work the pump. He had seen two small
figures in the upstairs window. Letting anyone burn
wasn't his way.

Slocum kicked in the door and reeled back as the
heat surged out to meet him. After the first blast, it
cooled enough for him to slip inside. He pulled his hat
down as far as he could to protect his face, then ran for
the stairs. Tiny flames danced the entire length of the
staircase. He went up carefully, the boards beneath his
feet weakened by the blaze.

At the top of the stairs his entire world became a small room surrounded by fire and smoke. He dropped to his knees and crawled; a scant foot of air near the floor was breathable.

"Where are you?" he shouted above the roar of the fire. "I want to get you out of here!"

A baby cried. Slocum crawled halfway down the hall until he came to a heavy wooden door to one of the sleeping rooms. Spinning around on his back, he kicked out and knocked open the door. The entire door panel fell into the room. Fire had weakened it. And fire was rapidly sapping Slocum's strength. He fought to get into the room.

The sound of the baby crying gave him new strength. On the floor lay an older child, a boy seven or eight years old. A woman was sprawled across the bed. Beside her a man dressed in the worn corduroy of a miner had passed out from the smoke.

Slocum sucked in what air he could, rose, and grabbed a chair. He heaved it through the window, then leaned out. The smoke took away his voice, but Tiny had been watching for him.

"Slocum, you stupid son of a bitch! Get out of there! The whole damned building's ready to collapse!"

"Get ready, Tiny," Slocum managed to sputter out. He grabbed the boy under the arms and spun him around. The limp form proved harder to move than if the boy had been awake and struggling. Slocum shoved him out and dropped him. Tiny might catch him. He might not. The boy was better off either way.

The woman went next. And then Slocum got his arms around the man and heaved him to the window sill.

"Hurry up, Slocum," yelled Tiny. "The woman and boy are all right. You get out of there right now!"

Slocum shoved the man out the window. His falling weight proved too much for Tiny. The giant staggered and fell under the load and didn't move. Slocum grabbed the still crying baby and held it in his arms. His shirt smoldered in places and his pants had caught fire at the cuffs.

When a bullet in his gunbelt went off from the heat, Slocum knew he had overstayed his welcome. He swung his long legs out and over the window sill. The once-sturdy frame under him began to creak and protest. He jumped. The impact when he hit the ground wasn't bad, but he had the baby in his arms. He tucked his head down and rolled, protecting the baby as he crashed into Tiny and the man still atop him.

Lying on the ground, stunned by the fall, Slocum found himself in a peculiar state. His mind worked fine. His body refused to budge. He heard others running up. He felt hands taking the baby from his arms. Even Tiny's voice did not bring control back to him. Slocum just lay on the ground, unable to move.

When a bucket of hot water was dashed in his face, Slocum jerked about and then managed to sit up. His arms and legs were as limp as wet wash rags. Two men dragged him away from the National Hotel just as the roof crashed in and sent sparks and flames shooting a hundred feet into the air.

"Sit and take it easy. Damn, I never seen a man do anything that stupid before," said Tiny. "Or that brave. And here I was thinkin' that you was just lucky, knocking me out like you done the other day. Me and Betsy'll be right proud having you stand up with us at the weddin'. Bring us good luck."

Slocum tried to rest. The sight of the fire spreading along the streets of Cripple Creek devouring the wood buildings disheartened him. But the miners fought back harder and the flames became smaller until they vanished.

All that was left in an hour was a soot-blackened brigade of firemen. They dragged in their hoses and carefully tended them. Slocum didn't have to be told what ran through each man's mind. They had to keep the hoses and pumps in good condition, because there would be another fire. Maybe not tomorrow, but sometime. The conditions in the District were such that it wasn't possible to build a fireproof structure.

Slocum wondered if that would ever be possible.

He looked up at the man towering above him. The man shuffled his feet and embarrassment etched deep lines in his face.

"You Slocum?" the man asked.

Slocum allowed that he was. "Do I know you?" he asked.

"You went into the hotel and got me and the wife and children out. The smoke made me pass out. Don't know if that's what happened to Sarah. Reckon so."

"You were lucky I saw you."

"The boy didn't pass out right away. Must have been him you saw." The man had more to say and struggled to find the words.

Slocum got to his feet. The man thrust out his hand for Slocum to take. "I ain't good at speeches. Thank you for saving us. We'd have been goners without you risking your life."

"Hell," boomed Tiny, slapping Slocum on the back. "He only did it so's he wouldn't have to take his turn at the pump."

"Is everyone going to recover?" Slocum asked.

"Sarah's still coughing a mite but the kids are hale and hearty. Uh, if there's anything I can ever do—"

"Just you stay out of burning buildings next time," said Slocum. The gratitude made him as uncomfortable as it did the man he'd saved. He shrugged it off.

Slocum looked past the man and Tiny and saw a familiar figure slipping away into the shadows. For a few seconds, Slocum's tired brain fought to identify the silhouette. Then it came to him. His hand flashed to his Colt and he checked the load. Slocum knocked two cartridges from the cylinder and replaced them when his inspection found suspect leakage on the bases from the primer.

"What's wrong, Slocum?" asked Tiny. "What you fixin' to go and do now?"

"I saw an old friend. Just want to have a few words with him."

Tiny stared at the Colt in Slocum's hand. "You want help with this fellow?" he asked. "There's got to be looters come swoopin' down on Cripple Creek like buzzards huntin' an easy meal. You spot one of them?"

"Help these people find a place to stay. If the Golconda's still standing, find blankets and put them in the back room."

"You want me to ask Jacobson?"

"Forget Jacobson," he said. "Do it. And see if anybody else who's needing shelter wants to sleep in the saloon." Slocum could be free with Jacobson's property. The owner wasn't in any position to complain. He might have one of the few buildings left intact in Cripple Creek.

Slocum pushed past the man and took off at a trot in pursuit of the man he had seen—the road agent who had robbed him on the stage coming up to Cripple Creek. Slocum tried to remember the man's name, then decided it wasn't worth the effort. When they'd both ridden with Quantrill, many of the men used summer names. When the season changed they'd be called something else and the reward posters would name an alias.

He stooped at the end of the alleyway and coughed when he got a lungful of smoke from a smoldering building. Most of the frames stood but the clapboard walls had been burned to ash. Through this destruction Slocum saw shadows moving across shadows. Like the wind, he pursued.

Getting his forty dollars back from the road agent wasn't what he had in mind. Putting the end to a career of death and destruction ranging back to the War was.

The raids with Quantrill had left too many towns looking like Cripple Creek. For a brief instant Slocum wondered if the highwayman had set the fire that reduced Cripple Creek to this smoking debris. He shook off the notion. What would the man have to gain? When they had ridden with Quantrill and Bloody Bill Anderson and the others, it had been war. Sherman had scorched Georgia and left a burned streak through the heart of a great state.

What they had done in the name of the Confederacy hadn't been any prettier.

Slocum slid his Colt from the holster and cocked it. The sound of the hammer coming back made him jump. The noise came as loud as a gunshot. He tried to calm himself. The fire had spooked him, rescuing the family from the burning hotel hadn't helped put him in an easy mood.

Slocum felt as if every nerve in his body was a steel wire pulled taut. The slightest movement set the wires to humming. He vibrated, jerking around, on edge, ready for a fight with the man sporting the white scar across his forehead.

"It's all done. The boss will like the way it looks. There's nothing to connect us with it." The soft whisper blasted across Slocum's consciousness like summer thunder. He edged forward to get a look at the man speaking.

Two men stood beside the smoking ruins of the land office. A white scar gleamed in pale moonlight streaking down from the crest of the mountains to the east.

"The others are out at the claim. We done good this time, Dex."

Dexter Morgan. The name seared itself like a brand in Slocum's memory. Dexter Morgan had matched Quantrill atrocity for atrocity.

Slocum moved to cover both men.

"There's not much left here. Good work." Dexter Morgan kicked through the land office rubble and nodded in appreciation. Slocum had the gut feeling that this gang of highwaymen might have set the fire, after all.

But why? These two didn't look intent on looting. They prowled around poking in the ashes.

"Which one gets your head blown off first?" Slocum asked, his weapon up and aimed.

Both men went for their guns. Slocum fired without hesitation. His heavy .45 slug caught the robber Morgan had spoken to high in the shoulder. The impact spun him around and threw him to the ground. Slocum worked the hammer on his Colt and got off another round before Morgan cleared his holster. The road agent grunted and doubled over, but his six-shooter kept coming out of its holster. Before Slocum could fire a third time, Dexter Morgan's pistol was out and blazing with astonishing accuracy.

Slocum dived for cover behind a charred beam. One bullet crashed into it and split the wood.

"Been a while, Dex," Slocum called. "You recognized me when you held up the stage."

"Son of a bitch. It *is* you," the man cried. He fired twice more, keeping Slocum down.

Slocum came to his knees and sent more lead winging after Morgan. But it was in vain. The night swallowed the man as it had so many times when they had gone on raids for Quantrill.

Slocum knocked out the spent brass and reloaded. Only then did he check the outlaw he'd shot down.

A sea of mud surrounded the man. Slocum rolled him over. The bullet had caught the man in the shoulder and had severed an artery. The mud had been formed from a mixture of blood and dirt.

Slocum went hunting. Dex Morgan left his own trail of blood. Slocum didn't think the outlaw's wound was too severe. As he tracked Morgan, the amount of blood decreased until it vanished entirely. In the wan moonlight Slocum wasn't able to keep on the outlaw's trail.

Disgusted, he shoved his pistol back into his holster and went back to the land office. To his surprise the outlaw's body had vanished. Slocum knelt and looked at the ground. Several men had come by and taken it away—in the direction of the Golconda.

Slocum walked toward the saloon, ready for anything. To his surprise, he found a dozen men laboring to load bodies into a wagon bed. He hadn't expected the citizens to get to work this fast to take care of the dead and dying.

"Hey, Slocum, there you are!" called Tiny. Betsy hung on his arm. The expression on their faces told Slocum that more bad news was on the way.

"Did they haul in a body from over at the land office?" Slocum asked. He indicated the men laboring to clear the streets of the dead.

"May have. But that's not what we gotta tell you." Tiny's face screwed up in a wrinkled mass. "Hell, I ain't good at this. You tell him, Betsy."

Slocum waited for the woman to give him the news that Tiny couldn't. When it came, all Slocum could do was sink to the boardwalk and sit. The night had given him too many shocks.

"John, it's bad. I know you're friends with him and that makes it hard. Jonathan Barclay's dead. The boys just found him not fifty feet from here, up in the direction of Carbonate Hill." Betsy rested her hand on Slocum's shoulder. Tears glistened in her eyes. "And it wasn't the fire that killed him."

"Somebody gunned him down," Tiny blurted out. The giant miner looked stricken that anyone would harm a friend of Slocum's. "His body was still warm."

Slocum's thoughts ranged farther than Jonathan Barclay. The man had been dying, whether he admitted it to himself or not. The consumption chewed him up inside. He might be better off dead.

But what about Mina Barclay and her daughter?

Slocum had to see. He heaved himself to his feet and started off in the direction of their tent. It had been a long night and it would get even longer.

11

John Slocum trudged along, the stench of the burned town in his nostrils. Each footstep he took was harder than the one before. The closer he got to Carbonate Hill and telling Mina Barclay that her husband had been killed the more he felt the tiredness, both emotional and physical.

He had hoped that Betsy and Tiny had mistaken the body for Barclay. Slocum had checked. They hadn't. A clean bullet hole appeared at the back of Barclay's head. What was left of his face was identifiable—barely. There had been no chance for this to be accidental. Severe powder burns charring the hair showed that the killer had placed his gun less than a foot from Barclay's head before firing. Whoever had done it had committed cold-blooded murder.

Slocum's arms ached from turning the pump. His clothing had holes throughout from where tiny fires had started. His hair hung in sweat-lank strings and he felt as if he had been on a week-long binge and now paid the price.

The dull moonlight lit the path up the hill enough for him to make out the silhouette of Barclay's tent. No one

119

stirred. He took a deep breath and went the rest of the distance to the top.

"Mina?" he called out. "I got some bad news for you. This is John Slocum."

No answer. He went closer, hand on his six-shooter.

"Mina? Kitty? You in there?" He drew his pistol and used the barrel to push back the canvas flap door. The tent was pitch black inside. He strained for smell or sound that would show a bushwhacker lying in wait inside. Nothing. He didn't even hear anything that meant anyone was inside, Mina or killer.

Slocum entered slowly, being careful not to outline himself in the door. He prowled around in the dark, then found the coal-oil lamp and lit it with a lucifer from a box nearby. Pale yellow light filled the tent. The beds hadn't been slept in and no sign of either Mina or her daughter let Slocum know they were safe.

He sat down heavily on a bedroll, his body unable to go on. He tried to stretch out his sore muscles. He only produced waves of rolling pain. Slocum lay back, thinking to rest for a moment. Within seconds he was asleep.

Slocum came instantly awake, hand on Colt, when he heard rapid footfalls outside. He swung around, gun ready when the tent flap jerked back.

"Kitty!" he called.

The young girl stopped, then came into the tent. "That you, Mr. Slocum?"

"I have some bad news for your ma. Where is she?"

"They . . . they took it. They came and they took it all. Mama sent me to look for Papa, but I can't find him. And the whole town's been burned down and I don't know what to do." She burst into tears. Slocum found himself comforting the girl.

"What do you mean 'they came and took it all?' Who are you talking about?"

"I . . . I don't know who they are. About ten men. All of them had pistols and rifles and shotguns. They came to the claim and said it was theirs and we had to leave."

Slocum went cold inside. Claim jumpers had killed

Barclay and then gone out to the site and taken possession of it. With the fire so thoroughly destroying the land office, valuable records would be gone. Whoever had the most guns to protect a claim made the best case for it being theirs. Especially if the claim's rightful owner had a bullet in his skull.

"Papa had started to put down a shaft. He'd gone into the hillside almost twenty feet and had hit two veins," Kitty said. "He's real good using dynamite."

"What happened to your mother?"

"She told me to run and find Papa. I couldn't. I looked and looked, but the town's all burned up, and . . ." Kitty choked, wiped away tears, and then looked at Slocum, her eyes wide. "They said he was dead. They said my papa was dead. Is that so, Mr. Slocum?"

"That's why I came up here to talk to your mother. I didn't want her or you finding out like this."

"They said he'd been gunned down. Did the men at our mine do this to him?"

"May have," Slocum allowed. "Where's your mother?"

"She's holding them off at the mine."

"She's what!" Slocum shot to his feet, ignoring the twinges of pain. All he had were sore muscles. Mina Barclay had war on her hands. If she was still alive. Men who would backshoot an unarmed miner wouldn't think twice about gunning down a woman.

"She's got a rifle and she's inside the mineshaft trying to keep them away from our claim. With Papa dead, there's only us now, isn't there?"

Slocum looked around the tent for more ammunition. He found nothing. Barclay had never carried a gun; most miners couldn't afford one. There was no reason for him to keep ammunition in the tent if he didn't own a pistol.

"Where did she get the rifle?"

"She took it from one of the men. She hit him with a rock."

A fleeting smile crossed Slocum's lips. Mina Barclay had courage. She was a real fighter. But no one could hold off an organized gang of claim jumpers for long.

"Where's the dynamite your pa used?"

"At the mine," the girl said. Slocum cursed. Getting to it looked to be his only chance for driving off the claim jumpers. The only ammunition he had was in his gunbelt and the cylinder of his Colt. He had less than twenty rounds.

"How many men are there?"

"I don't know. A lot. Maybe as many as ten," Kitty told him.

Slocum was an expert shot. Being a sniper during the War had taught him the value of making every shot count, but he knew it was impossible to face down ten men with only twenty rounds. Even grabbing up fallen weapons and using them didn't afford him much more chance. And these weren't drunken miners out on a lark. They were killers.

Just like him.

He pushed through the tent flap and headed in the direction of the claim. He stopped and turned. Kitty Barclay followed him.

"Get on into Cripple Creek," he said, "and find Tiny. Tell him what you told me."

"The big man?"

"Him. Tell him what's going on at your pa's claim and tell him to bring ammunition."

Kitty was obviously torn between disobeying and going back to the claim and doing what she was told. Good sense prevailed.

"I'll hurry, Mr. Slocum. You're going to help Mama?"

"If I can," he said. Slocum didn't hold out much chance that the woman was still alive. Her being trapped in a mine meant that the ten men against her had an easy time of it. Mina Barclay wouldn't be able to move around or escape.

Only when he saw the girl going down the hill did

Slocum start for the claim. He didn't want Kitty Barclay caught up in the middle of a gunfight. By the time he reached the ravine to the north of Barclay's claim he heard sporadic gunfire. That meant good news. Mina Barclay still fought off the claim jumpers. How she had managed this, Slocum didn't know. But if anybody could, that determined woman was the one.

Slocum scouted the perimeter of the claim to see how many claim jumpers there were. Kitty might have missed one or two or she might have guessed too many. Unless they were used to it, people always exaggerated when being shot at. Even then, Slocum mistrusted estimates.

To his surprise, the girl had hit exactly the number of bushwhackers. Ten men scattered around the hillside all fired into the low mouth of a newly blasted mineshaft.

Slocum moved like a shadow as he came up behind one claim jumper. He swung his Colt in a sharp, vicious arc that connected with the back of the man's head. The sick crunch told him that the man wouldn't get up soon. Slocum took what ammunition the man had. It was only ten more rounds, but it helped. Every round counted.

Almost immediately he was discovered. A fusillade of bullets kicked up the dirt at his feet and sent rock splinters into his face as pieces of lead richocheted. He dodged from side to side, trying to take cover as best he could on the bare hillside.

"Who is it?" called out one of the claim jumpers. "One of those damned miners?"

Slocum located the source of the questions and ended the man's life with three well-placed shots.

"He got Jake. And where's—" Slocum cut off the inventory with three more shots that drove the man for cover. Slocum rolled and came to his knees. He reloaded. He had only two dozen rounds left.

A rifle report came from the mouth of the mineshaft. Mina's voice followed. "They've come to help. Jonathan's brought the whole damned town to stop you!" she cried.

"Your man's dead," came a voice Slocum recognized instantly. Dexter Morgan led the claim jumpers. It came as no surprise. When Slocum had finally identified the man, all the crimes made sense. If a cause of the fire was ever found, it could be laid at Morgan's feet. "I shot the son of a bitch myself."

Slocum decided there wasn't any way he could get a clean shot at Morgan. He had winged the man once tonight. A second shot wouldn't miss its target of the outlaw's putrid heart. But in thinking about Morgan he had neglected to protect his own back.

Slocum's carelessness allowed two of the claim jumpers to circle behind. They opened up, one with a rifle and the other with a shotgun. A piece of hot buckshot ripped through Slocum's left arm. He winced and rolled, ending up on his back. He emptied his Colt, not sure if he hit either of the men.

Eighteen rounds left. He was running low. Where was Tiny? Had Kitty reached town and found the giant? Slocum didn't want to consider the possibility that Tiny and Betsy had gone off somewhere and Kitty couldn't find him.

The situation at the Barclay claim was getting serious.

Dexter Morgan shouted, "Rush the mine. Now!"

Dark forms rose from the side of the hill and moved forward. Slocum fired slowly and accurately, emptying his Colt once more. He winged two of the men. From the way they shouted and carried on, neither was seriously hurt.

An even dozen rounds left. Six in his pistol, six in his gunbelt. He had two choices open. He could slip away and get help or he could try to help Mina Barclay.

Slocum rushed forward, dodging both the claim jumpers' bullets as well as Mina's.

"It's me—Slocum!" he shouted. "Let me get inside!"

"John?"

The woman's instant of hesitation was enough for Slocum to get into the mouth of the mine and swing around. He emptied his pistol again. This time he knew he ended the life of one claim jumper. The man jerked upright, stood for a moment, then sagged bonelessly.

Slocum had six rounds left.

"How much ammunition do you have?" he asked Mina.

"John, where's Jonathan? They said that he was dead."

"This is no time to discuss it."

"Then it *is* true. He's dead," she said in a monotone.

"We'll be dead, too, unless we stop them. How much ammunition do you have?"

"Only what I took off one of them." She held out a grimy hand. In it were three shells.

"And the rifle?"

"Empty. I'm not very good at reloading."

He snatched the shells and rifle from her hands and quickly slipped the rounds into the magazine. He levered the Winchester and got ready for the claim jumpers to attack. He didn't have long to wait. Dex Morgan sent his men straight up the hill in a frontal assault.

Slocum used the three rounds well, killing one and wounding another. That left him with only six shots, all in his Colt.

"We're in bad trouble, aren't we?" Mina asked. "I'd hoped that you would rescue me. I didn't want you to die with me."

"We're not dead yet. Kitty mentioned that your husband used dynamite to blast into the hill." He rolled over and reached out. His hand brushed against the mine's roof. The entire stoop was less than four feet high and was unshored. Unless he was careful, an explosion would bring tons of rock crashing down on them.

"There's a case back in the mine. I pushed it there. Jonathan had left it down the hill. When the claim jumpers came, I didn't want them being able to use it."

"You know how to set a blasting cap?" In the darkness Slocum saw the woman shake her head. "Get the dynamite. We're going to need it in a hurry." He peered out the mine and downhill. He saw tempting targets moving around there, but held his fire. The six remaining rounds would be needed soon.

Mina dragged back the small carton of dynamite sticks. Barclay had used most of them. Only ten sticks remained. Mina treated them as if they were likely to go off in her hand.

Slocum grabbed them roughly and found a ball of twine. He fastened the dynamite together in five two-stick bundles. Barclay had prepared blasting caps with fuses. Slocum stuck the cap-and-fuse into each bundle, then reached for a lucifer. His fingers brushed across only charred cloth. The vest pocket where he had carried the lucifers had been burned away in the fire.

He didn't ask Mina if she had a lucifer. There was no reason for the woman to carry any. He searched frantically through the case. Barclay was too good a miner to keep sensitive lucifers near the fuses and caps.

"Is there anything we can light the fuses with?" he asked Mina.

"I don't know. I don't think so."

Slocum looked out again. Dex Morgan had his men moving once more. They might have thought those trapped in the mine were out of ammunition—or they might not have cared. Dragging out the gunfight served only those defending the claim.

Slocum swung his Colt up and started to shoot, then stopped. He smiled slowly. He kept the six-shooter aimed downhill, but pulled out a bundle of dynamite. "Hold the fuse directly over the muzzle," he ordered Mina. "Don't flinch. When the fuse is lit, hand the dynamite to me."

"I should throw it," she said.

"Do as you're told." Slocum found a likely target, saw that Mina held the fuse where he'd told her, then fired. The bullet missed the claim jumper, but the flash from burning wadding and partially spent gunpowder set fire to the fuse.

Slocum snatched the dynamite from Mina and quickly held the fuse of another bundle to the first. Then he threw the first two sticks as hard as he could. Seconds later the earth shook from the explosion. By this time, Slocum had a third fuse lit. He tossed the second bundle.

He kept doing this until all five bundles had been thrown.

"Now what?" asked Mina, tears streaming down her grimy cheeks.

"We hope." Slocum wriggled to the mouth of the mine and looked downhill. He saw no movement. He had five rounds left. He decided to put them to good use. He motioned for the woman to stay inside the mine. Slocum slithered like a snake until he got to a large boulder a few yards from the mine. He pulled himself up and looked around from his protected vantage point.

Nothing moved in the night. His hearing was slightly impaired from the five explosions, but his night vision was excellent. He found each of the craters. He held his position until he was certain that Dexter Morgan's claim jumpers had fled.

Slocum holstered his Colt, shaking his head in wonder. He still had five rounds left.

"Come on out," he told Mina Barclay. "It's safe. They've turned tail and run."

She emerged from the mine, dress torn and face dirty. Slocum wondered if he had ever seen a more beautiful sight. He doubted it.

"What if they hadn't fled?" she asked. "What if the dynamite hadn't been enough?"

"We'd be dead," he said honestly. "But it worked. That's what matters."

The ringing in his ears had died down enough for him to hear the sound of horses' hooves on rock. He pushed her behind him, silently motioning for her to return to the mine.

He slipped his Colt from its holster and waited, hammer back and ready to resume the fight.

A swaybacked horse struggled up the hill under its ponderous load. Slocum relaxed.

"Tiny!" he called out. "Did you see any of them?"

"Haven't seen anyone. Heard explosions. Dynamite?"

"That's what I used to drive them off," said Slocum.

"Then there really was claim jumpers here like the little girl said." The giant miner got off his horse. The animal nickered in appreciation of losing such a weight on its back.

"They killed Jonathan Barclay and then came out to take his claim," and Slocum. "The leader is Dexter Morgan."

"Morgan. I heard of him. Don't rightly remember where."

"He's one mean son of a bitch," said Slocum. "Don't go tangling with him."

"You done all right against him."

"And nine others," added Mina.

Tiny cocked his head to the side and stared at her. "You the ma of that girl back in town? My Betsy's lookin' after her."

"I'd better go see to Kitty," the woman said.

"No need. Betsy's able to take care of her for a while. She's sleepin' like a baby." Tiny paused, then added, "Hearin' that her pa's dead took the stuffin' right out of her." Tiny apparently didn't consider the effect his words would have on Mina Barclay.

She sagged. Slocum caught her and held her up. "I'll get her back to her tent. You and Betsy will look after Kitty?"

"Sure will, Slocum. The way Betsy's taken to the kid makes me wonder if our gettin' hitched ain't good timin'."

"Mrs. Barclay will be by tomorrow to get Kitty. You staying at the Golconda?"

"Upstairs. You look after the widow, won't you, Slocum?"

Slocum said nothing. Tiny mounted his protesting horse and headed back toward Cripple Creek. Slocum looked around the claim site and decided there wasn't anything more to do here. If the claim jumpers returned, they could have it. The sheriff had to return soon. Slocum would get the matter settled then.

His arm around Mina Barclay's waist, Slocum headed back for the tent atop Carbonate Hill. It had been one hell of a night.

12

Slocum and Mina Barclay walked back to her tent in silence, each at the bottom of a personal well of thought. They hiked up the hill and stood awkwardly in front of the tent flap.

"You look a fright," Mina said finally. "Come in for a few minutes. Let me fix you a cup of coffee."

"Sounds good," Slocum said. "I hope you don't mind, but I already took a nap in your bed."

"What?" The woman's startled expression caused Slocum to laugh.

"Before Kitty came and told me about your trouble at the claim, I came up here. After fighting the fire in Cripple Creek, I was so dog tired I sat down. Then I lay down. Then I was sound asleep. One thing just led to another."

"The fire?" she asked. "What has been happening? I know this is a terribly primitive town, but so much is going on. And I don't like a bit of it."

Slocum told her about the fire and how he and Tiny had manned the water pump. He left out telling her about the family he had rescued from the National Hotel. It embarrassed him to hear people go on about how he was some kind of hero. At the moment, Slocum didn't feel like a hero. He felt like homemade shit.

"No wonder your clothes are all tattered and burned. You deserve some reward. Let me give you some of Jonathan's clothing. He was smaller than you, but I can let out a few seams. After all, he won't be needing them any longer."

Mina realized what she had said and burst out crying. Slocum found himself with his arms around her, comforting her, trying to convince her that everything would be all right. But he knew that it wouldn't. Jonathan Barclay lay dead from a murderer's bullet. Claim jumpers had tried to take the mine. The town of Cripple Creek had barely survived a disastrous fire. Nothing was right.

How could he soothe the woman when there was so damned little to give her in the way of hope?

"You and Kitty don't have to worry. That mine's worth something. You can sell it and be well off. Nothing'll bring back your husband, but at least he didn't leave you broke."

"John," Mina said softly, her face buried in his shoulder, "my husband was never much of a prospector. It was pure blind luck that he found this vein."

"Luck is better than skill at times," Slocum said.

Mina pushed back from Slocum and brushed away the tears. "Let me get to work on those clothes for you. You can't go out looking like that."

"No one will notice," he said, but he detected something more in what the woman was saying. "You want me to get out of these rags?"

"Yes," she said in a small voice. "I need you, John. You're a good man. I need a good man to help me. I know it's weak, but . . ."

He took her in his arms and gently kissed her. The aches and pains receded. The tiredness he had been feeling all the way back to the tent vanished. Passion rose within him as he kissed her lips, felt her body moving against his, thrilled to her hands working up and down his back.

"I need you so much!" she exclaimed. Her eager

fingers worked at the buttons of his shirt. Some popped and went rolling off in the dirt. Neither Slocum nor Mina noticed. She got his shirt off and let him hang up his gunbelt.

"You're so dirty. Let me clean you off."

"Mina," he said, not sure if he ought to continue. He wanted her. She was a beautiful woman, but she was also confused. Her husband had been murdered this night. She had been shot at and threatened. Did she know what she was doing, or did she act out of shock?

Slocum sighed at the woman's gentle touch as she began washing off the grime from the fire. She washed his face and neck and chest and back, then moved around to face him. She kissed him. There wasn't a trace of confusion in what she did then.

"I need you tonight, John. Really, I do. I can't be alone."

"It doesn't have to be this way."

"Yes, it does."

Her hunger startled him. She kissed him so hard that she pushed him back onto the thin pallet that served as her bed. Somehow she managed to open her dress and skin out of the blouse. Her bare breasts rubbed against Slocum's chest, the nipples hardening. Her heart pounded fiercely beneath her breast. Slocum cupped the mound of tender flesh in his hand and squeezed gently.

Mina sobbed with need. He moved so that he could kiss the very tip. The coral-colored fleshy bead throbbed with vitality. He took it between his lips, sucked, teased it with his teeth, ran his tongue over it. Mina Barclay writhed on the bed now, her moans becoming more insistent.

"Don't stop, John. I want it. I *want* you!"

He moved from the left breast to the right and repeated all that he had done. By this time Mina's hips were rising from the bed and she moved urgently to get the rest of her dress off. She wriggled and kicked and got free.

She looked up at him and said nothing. The expres-

sion on her face let him know that this was what she
needed—and Slocum realized it was what he needed,
too. He worked at the buttons on his denims and snaked
them off.

Mina pounced on him like a puma stalking a rabbit.
She took him in hand and squeezed gently. His manhood stiffened until it was painful. The woman stroked
from the thick base to the tip and ran her fingers over
the purpled hood before kissing it.

Slocum moved down between her legs. Mina opened
for him. For a moment, Slocum hung poised. The
woman's insistence convinced him that he was not only
doing what he wanted but was doing what they both
needed. His hips swung forward.

Mina moaned and reached down to guide him into
her. The sudden entry took away their breath. Slocum
hung above her, stiff arms supporting him, half sunk
into the well of her femininity, not moving. He savored
the intimate sensation of being totally surrounded by her
hot, clinging sheath of female flesh. He began to throb
and jerk and strain against her.

"Move, John, deep, all the way. In, I need you inside
me, *inside!*" Her sentence ended with a shriek as he
buried himself in her. Slocum again stopped, enjoying
the feel of her. Then he slowly began to pull out. The
sweet agony was almost more than he could bear.

He never hesitated. He slid forward again, faster,
harder. Mina shuddered like a leaf in a high wind. Her
hands roved restlessly up and down his arms. Her sharp
fingernails digging into his flesh.

Slocum began moving faster. The tempo of his lovemaking increased until he thrust frantically, all attempt
to control himself lost. He wanted her, he needed her,
he was going to have her!

"Yes, John, don't stop, don't you dare stop!" she
sobbed out. Her hips began rising to meet his powerful
inward thrusts. Mina ground her crotch into his when he
fully buried himself. And she squeezed down tight with
her inner muscles as he tried to retreat.

The woman's excitement always betrayed her. No matter how much she wanted Slocum to remain inside her, he could always pull out. Faster and faster they slammed together, their sweaty bodies linking intimately.

"Now, oh yes, now!" she shrieked. Her back arched and she clasped her hands around Slocum's neck and her slender legs around his waist. The grip was so powerful that Slocum couldn't escape—and he didn't want to.

When she relaxed a mite, he began thrusting harder than before. Again she screamed out her desires. This time his seed spilled inside her. Like a mineshaft collapsing she held him firmly until he began to deflate.

Slocum sank forward, his chest pressing down on her firm breasts. He rolled to one side. Their arms fit naturally around one another and they lay with their faces only inches apart.

"Everything is happening so fast," Mina said.

"Sorry. Didn't mean for it to be over this quick," he said. She laughed and snuggled closer.

"That wasn't what I meant. That was fine, John. Really. I meant Jonathan and coming to Cripple Creek and the holdup on the stage and *everything.*"

He sensed that she was close to losing control over her brittle emotions. He held her as tightly as he could to reassure her that she had nothing to fear.

"We should never have come out here. I wanted to stay in Kansas City, but Jonathan sounded so enthusiastic about Cripple Creek. Maybe he only wrote like that to make me think he was all right."

"The consumption," said Slocum. "How long did he have to live?"

"He wouldn't talk about it, but from his coughing fits, I doubt he could have lived much longer. He never took medicine for it. Maybe a quick death is better than dying by inches."

"No death is good. There are too many things to live for."

"Oh," she said with surprising harshness. "Name one."

Slocum looked into her brown eyes and said, "You. I could die for you. Even more important, I could live for you."

"Jonathan couldn't," Mina said. "He had a dream. That was more important to him than me or Kitty or anything else in life." She fell silent. After a long pause, she kissed him tenderly. "What's your dream? What do you live for?"

"Believe it or not, I've been thinking on that," Slocum admitted. "Can't rightly give an answer. But with you, there might be more of a chance to find the answer."

Neither spoke then. In a few minutes Mina slept deeply, her head resting on Slocum's shoulder. It took him longer to fall asleep. He worked through all that had happened since he came to Cripple Creek. Some was bad, some good. Maybe the best was what had just occurred between him and Mina.

But getting to this point had been hard and painful. Her husband had been killed and Slocum had found Dexter Morgan. Slocum had run off claim jumpers and seen Morgan leading them. The stagecoach robbery had been done by Morgan. All the viciousness in the District tied in with that man.

Slocum would end Morgan's career in crime.

He fell asleep in Mina Barclay's arms dreaming of Morgan and Quantrill and fire and bullets.

"They fit a damned sight better than any I've worn in a long time," Slocum marvelled. He looked at the shirt and trousers Mina had fit on him. Jonathan Barclay had been smaller and less muscular, but letting out a seam here and there had done wonders.

"I've got to be getting on into town," Slocum said. "I doubt if Oscar Jacobson wants me around any more, since I didn't show up for work last night."

"But the town burned down!" Mina exclaimed. "Oh,

you're just joking. Sometimes I wonder about you, John Slocum."

"Wasn't kidding. Not exactly. Jacobson doesn't strike me as the kind of man who lets his employees off a night, no matter what's happened."

"I doubt if the Golconda was even open."

Slocum smiled broadly. "I think it was. I told Tiny that anyone who needed to could sleep there. The whole damned place was probably filled to overflowing."

"You don't think this Jacobson person would appreciate your charity? You shouldn't work for someone who lacks even the most elementary courtesy towards his fellow man," Mina said with conviction.

"I'll see that Kitty's brought back all right," he said. "You don't have to make the trip into town."

"I will. She's my responsibility."

Together they left the tent and started down Carbonate Hill. New tents had sprung up on the slopes like toadstools growing in the moist night air. Those who had been burned out of their houses in Cripple Creek had moved to the poorer section at the edge of town to live. Slocum decided this was good for Mina. Neighbors this close would keep her mind off her own miseries.

"The town is a fright," Mina said, staring at the charred remains of the buildings. Already men worked to tear down the ruined walls and put up new ones. In a week there would be scant sign that a fire had ravaged the town. In a month no one would bet on there ever having been a fire unless they had seen it with their own eyes.

"I . . . you go on in, John. I don't think it's proper for me to go into a saloon." Mina hesitated for a moment, then said, "I've changed my mind. If my daughter is there, I ought to be, also."

Slocum held the swinging door back for the woman as she entered, trying to look confident. Men sprawled on the floor all the way to the back room, some sleeping, others sitting up and looking dazed. They had fought the fires and lost all their belongings. Slocum had nothing but sympathy for them.

He wondered if he should tell them his suspicions about Dex Morgan setting the fire. He decided not to. He wanted Morgan for himself.

"Slocum!" bellowed Tiny. Kitty peered out from behind his huge bulk. The girl squealed with joy when she saw her mother and bolted into the woman's arms.

"These folks surely do appreciate you lettin' 'em sleep in the saloon, Slocum. There aren't that many other usable buildings still standing," said Tiny.

"Did Jacobson have anything to say about it?"

Tiny smiled. "He did, but I throwed him out on his ass. He fired Betsy, but that's jist fine with us. Threatened to fire me from the mine until Frank Dennis told him all the Free Coinage Union members would walk out if he did, which ain't much of a threat since we'll probably strike anyway. Jacobson didn't say much after that."

"What's left in town?" asked Slocum.

"I looked around. Some are already rebuilding the places in the best shape. There wasn't much in the way of people dyin'. Maybe ten died."

"The claim jumpers moved in fast. I think that they set the fire to destroy the land office records." Slocum had kept his voice down but several men nearby overheard.

They bellowed and roared at this until Tiny outshouted the lot of them.

"If what you say's true," said Tiny, "we got a necktie party to plan. I'm not letting any road agents think they can take over Cripple Creek like this. Why, that'd make them my neighbor!"

Tiny's logic escaped Slocum, but the big man's concern was real. Slocum said, "I want to go through the ruins of the land office and see what can be salvaged. It might be that the deeds are intact. I remember seeing the clerk put Barclay's claim into a sturdy cabinet. It might have kept away the worst of the heat."

Slocum, Mina and Kitty, Tiny, and several others went to where the land office had stood only the day before. The timbers still smoldered. Slocum decided that the only way of uncovering the truth was to dig. He grabbed a long board and began poking through the still-hot ashes. Mina soon joined him. When Tiny and the others pitched in, they located the cabinet where the deeds had been filed.

Tiny grunted as he heaved the big box up and out of the ashes. He deposited it in the center of the street. The men gathered around when Slocum opened the drawer. The sides of the box had felt hot; he worried that a fire might blaze up when the drawer opened and exposed the contents to the air.

All he found inside were tightly packed files that had been charred around the edges.

"They're readable," he declared. A whoop of triumph went up in the crowd. Many of the men had independent claims that might have been lost if the deeds had been destroyed.

Slocum began pawing through the files. The heat had turned the pages brittle. He let Mina separate the sheets.

"What's going on here?" demanded Oscar Jacobson. The man had ridden up, two gunmen with him. "You, Slocum, what are you doing?"

"Looking for the clerk's records. These men—" He looked at Mina and added, "and women need proof of their claims. We found the box with the deeds in it."

The expression crossing Jacobson's face puzzled Slocum. It combined surprise and amusement.

"What's your interest, Slocum? You're not a miner. You're supposed to be working for me over at the Golconda."

"I do have an interest," Slocum said, his cold green eyes fixed on Jacobson. "I'm part owner of Jonathan Barclay's mine. He gave me five percent."

"That's right," chimed in one of the men gathered. "I heard Barclay say so. Slocum gave him the money to file the deed and assay some ore."

"John," Mina said. "The deed's not here. Jonathan's filing is missing!"

"So's mine!" came an immediate cry of outrage. "And mine!" "Mine, too!" A dozen men rummaged through the deeds, trying futilely to find their land deeds.

"Looks like most of the profitable independent prospectors are included in what's missing," Tiny observed. He walked over to Jacobson. The giant's head was only a foot below the mounted Jacobson's. "You wouldn't happen to know anything about this strange coincidence, now would you, Mr. Jacobson?"

"Funny that you should mention it," said Jacobson. His expression was one of triumph. "I happen to remember that the clerk said some deeds had been sent over to the bank earlier today. Might be in the vault."

"Why would the clerk separate his records?" Mina asked.

Slocum gripped her by the arm to silence her. He didn't like the sound of what Jacobson said. The claim jumpers had been well organized. From what he remembered of Dexter Morgan, the man carried out orders well, but didn't do too well when placed on his own. Dex Morgan might not be the leader of the claim jumpers.

Slocum figured he didn't have far to look if somebody else headed the band of outlaws. He unhooked the thong on the hammer of his Colt. It might be worth the effort to end the thieving here and now.

His motion had been seen by the two gunmen riding with Jacobson. One jerked out a sawed-off shotgun. The other got a Remington from his saddle sheath and levered in a shell.

"Don't go getting my boys riled, Slocum."

"When do you suppose we could look at the deeds that are in the bank vault?" he asked, knowing the answer.

"Right now is as good as any. If you gentlemen— and you, too, ma'am—want to come to the bank, we can settle this matter quickly enough."

Jacobson spurred his horse on ahead. Slocum and the others trailed behind. Slocum was acutely aware of the two gunmen following. They hadn't put away either shotgun or rifle.

"What's going on, John?" asked Mina. "Why did the clerk send the deeds over to the bank?"

"Let's wait and ask," said Slocum. But he knew the answers to the woman's questions already. What Tiny had said would prove to be right.

They entered the bank. The land office clerk worked behind a makeshift desk at one side of the lobby. The bank had a few scorch marks on the outer walls, but had weathered the fire well.

"Get these folks the deeds you put away for me," Jacobson said.

"Why, Mr. Jacobson?" asked the clerk.

"Because I said so, damn it!" the man flared. The clerk scurried away like a frightened rabbit.

When he came back with a box, Tiny jerked it from his hands and dropped it on the desk. The giant ripped through the contents, passing the files out.

"Here, here it is!" cried Mina. "I remember the claim number. Jonathan said it was his lucky number." She quickly scanned it and her face clouded over. "This isn't the deed. This one's—"

"That one's registered by Mr. Jacobson."

"So's mine!" went up the chorus.

All the deeds had been rewritten with Oscar Jacobson as the owner.

"This is why I had the deeds brought to the bank," Jacobson said smoothly. "Since all of them are mine, I wanted to protect them. It was sheer chance that fire broke out and destroyed the land office."

"You had the records changed, you lying bastard!" shouted a miner. A solid *chuck!* followed by the sound of a body falling caused Slocum to spin, hand on pistol. The gunman with the rifle had slugged the miner. The other held the shotgun aimed squarely at his midsection.

If Slocum had drawn, both barrels would have torn him in half.

"There's nothing wrong with the claims, Mr. Jacobson. You recorded them all," said the clerk. His frightened look told the story.

"Of course there's nothing wrong with the claims," Jacobson said.

"You stole my husband's claim," Mina Barclay said savagely. "It wouldn't surprise me one iota if you had him killed, too!"

"Ma'am, that's a serious accusation. I know you're upset over your recent loss. You'd better not go spreading malicious lies about me, though, or I'll have to take you to court."

"You stole my claim!"

"This is all legal. It will hold up in court," Jacobson said coldly. "I have the deeds, I own the claims." He gestured for his gunmen to clear the others out of the bank.

"John, don't let him do this. He's trying to steal the mine!"

"There's nothing I can do, Mina." Slocum took the woman by the arm and pulled her from the bank.

"You can't just give in like that!" she raged. "We've got to fight!"

"You're right," he said, "but not against men with shotguns aimed at us."

"Oh!" She stamped her foot. "There must be some way." A look of determination crossed her face. "There's a lawyer in town. I heard tell of him coming in from Denver. I'll see him right away. I'm not going to let Jacobson take *my* mine!"

She stalked off. Slocum started to call after her, but decided to save his breath. In the mood she was in, no amount of talking would convince her that she was on a fool's errand.

Slocum and the others started back toward the Golconda. He had to get his gear out of the back room and see if the few precious ounces of gold dust were still where he'd hidden them. He didn't think Jacobson would want to pay him for the work he had already done at the saloon.

13

Slocum heaved a sigh of relief. The small pouch of gold dust was still where he had hidden it. He dipped the tip of his finger in the gold flakes and held it up. The sheen was unlike anything else in the world. Gold gave beauty and riches and power. He rubbed the dust off his finger and back into the bag before tucking it away safely. Slocum finished packing his gear and heaved it to his shoulder.

With any luck, he could buy a horse and be on his way in a bit. The only business he had to settle was with Dexter Morgan. But Slocum stopped and thought. Did he really want to drift on west? Nothing held him in Cripple Creek. Nothing.

The more he told himself this, the more Mina Barclay came to mind. She would get nowhere talking to the lawyer from Denver. Slocum knew that Jacobson was a smooth operator. He would not let a lawyer practice in Cripple Creek without having him on the payroll. Anyone confident enough to burn down half the town to destroy the land office records had already planned ahead. Oscar Jacobson had his sights set on taking over all the gold mining in the District.

The notion that Jacobson told Morgan what to do

rankled. Slocum wasn't so sure he could just ride out of town and let such snakes live. Holding up stages wasn't that bad; Slocum had done it enough times himself, when the need arose. He considered his loss irritating and nothing more. But claim jumping was another thing altogether.

"Hey, Slocum," Tiny called from across the saloon. "You fixin' to move on?"

"Didn't think Jacobson would want me on the payroll after what just happened."

"You got a point. What you plannin' to do?" The giant miner peered at him with interest.

"I've got a score to settle with Dex Morgan. Finding him isn't going to be a cakewalk."

"I heard there's more trouble brewin' with Frank Dennis and the other union members. Somebody's stirrin' them up something fierce." Tiny smiled. "I'm even thinkin' of joinin' up, after they stood up for me and all. Dennis has got a point about us hanging together. No way we're gonna get a red cent out of Jacobson if 'n we don't."

"Three dollars for a shift isn't too much to ask," Slocum said, but his mind went to other concerns. The claim jumping had been well organized. The records had been removed and falsified before the fire had been set. Morgan and his men had known exactly where to go to take possession of Barclay's claim and others.

Why did Jacobson allow the union to agitate? Jacobson stood only to lose if the Independence Mine shut down for any length of time. Even owning all the outlying mines, he couldn't equal the gold taken from the immense Battle Mountain mine. It looked to Slocum as if Jacobson let his grip slip on the Independence and concentrated too much on the claim jumping.

That was a stupid move. And he didn't think Oscar Jacobson was a stupid man.

"They are marchin' down the street now," said Tiny.

Slocum pulled back from his thoughts. "The miners? Where are they going?"

"The Independence Mine office is still standing, sort of," the miner said. "Dennis figured that this was the time to make his big drive. The men are furious about the fire. Didn't take much to get them to come out of the mines."

Slocum and Tiny went to the corner of Second and Bennett and watched as the miners shouted slogans and threw rocks at the Independence office. Slocum turned from the crowd and studied the surrounding buildings. Few of them had been seriously touched by the fire. Many had sustained some damage when sparks from the fire had landed on wood shingle roofs. Other than this minor scorching, the buildings looked to be in good shape.

"Any of these owned by Jacobson?" Slocum asked.

"The buildings? Reckon most are the property of the mine," said Tiny. He moved back and forth like a circus elephant, swaying in indecision. He finally broke the spell. "Got to join them, Slocum. You comin' along?"

"Go on. I'll just watch a while longer."

Tiny nodded and lumbered off to add his voice to the din raised by the other miners. Slocum was more interested in the second-floor window of an office across the street from the Independence Mine headquarters. A man stood in the window, thumbs hooked in a fancy bright red silk vest. Slocum had walked out to where he could get a better view when a second figure crowded into the window to watch the miners.

The second man was Oscar Jacobson. The two men talked for a few minutes before Jacobson vanished from sight. He never came out the front. Slocum guessed he had left by the back way.

"John! There you are." Mina Barclay strode up, determination and anger written on her face. "I have just spoken to the lawyer. That man made me so mad!"

"That him in the window?" Slocum pointed to the portly man in the red vest.

"Yes, that's Mr. Grassley. What a positively annoying man he is!"

Slocum half-listened as Mina recited all the legal reasons lawyer Grassley had given about the difficulty in proving ownership of the Barclay claim.

"It all boiled down to Jacobson having a deed and the clerk backing him up. That's it. They've stolen the mine!"

"Jonathan got a copy of the deed. It had the clerk's name written on it. Might be hard convincing a judge bought and paid for by Jacobson that it is legal, but it's a place to start."

"The duplicate deed? Why, I don't know what Jonathan could have done with it," she said, frowning. "I didn't even know he had a copy."

The crowd turned rowdy now. Several thrown rocks found targets inside the mine offices. The windows had long since been knocked out. When gunfire sounded from inside the office, Slocum grabbed Mina and swung her around.

"Stay down. This won't last too long, unless I miss my guess."

The gunfire died down in a few seconds. Few of the miners carried weapons other than the rocks they had picked up on the march to the office. Who had shot into the office seemed a great mystery. Frank Dennis went through the crowd demanding to know.

"We're seeing a carefully planned riot," said Slocum. "Nobody's going to be hurt. Not yet . . . not unless Jacobson needs it."

"What are you saying, John?"

"It took me a spell to puzzle this out. I couldn't understand what Jacobson gained from having the Independence shut down by labor trouble. Wouldn't surprise me if he wasn't behind it. He might be paying Dennis for all the agitating."

"Why? He's part owner. The gold will be cut off if no miners are at work."

"What if Jacobson convinces the other owners back in Denver to sell to him for a fraction of the mine's worth? He ends up owning it completely and doesn't have to pay much for it."

"But the miners . . ."

"When he gets control, Jacobson looks like a knight in shining armor by giving the miners their pay raise. And why not? He can afford it if he owns an entire mountain of gold instead of just a few pebbles."

"The other owners would see what he's doing."

"Not if a slick city lawyer named Grassley did all the dirty work. I saw Jacobson up in the lawyer's office. Those two are in cahoots."

"Jacobson will end up owning Cripple Creek!" Mina exclaimed.

"Looks like he's got a good start. I've been thinking about how the fire spread, too. Might be more to it than just burning down the land office. The Independence Mine offices are still standing. It'd be interesting to see if Jacobson's competitors weren't the ones who suffered most."

"The Nugget Saloon was untouched."

"It's only a few yards from the Golconda. Jacobson isn't going to cut off his nose to spite his face. He may be very close to being the only real power in Cripple Creek."

Mina Barclay clenched her fists so tightly that her knuckles turned white. "He isn't going to steal Jonathan's mine. My husband died for the claim. I can't let Jacobson get away with it."

Slocum settled down, his back against a wood wall, and watched the ebb and flow of the union miners in the street. So much shouting and rock throwing might spook the other owners of the Independence Mine. The threat of another fire might work, too.

And all so legal. The crooked lawyer in the red silk vest made it that way.

Where would Jonathan Barclay keep his copy of the land deed?

"The deed," Slocum said suddenly. "It's not in your tent?"

"No, I don't think so," Mina said.

"The only other place a man like Jonathan would consider for a hiding place is the mine itself. He blasted powerful fast into the hillside. Is there somewhere inside the tunnel that he might have stashed the deed for safekeeping?"

"I don't know. The only time I was in the mine was yesterday, and I was doing more shooting than looking."

"There's going to be a ring of claim jumpers around the mine," Slocum said. "Now that they ran us off, they're not going to let us back on the property."

"They haven't run *me* off," Mina said.

"No, I reckon not. Me, either."

"What are you going to do, John?"

"A frontal assault doesn't make much sense when you're outgunned and outnumbered. Being sneaky is the best I can do." He laughed. "They're going to be sorry they ever tangled with me."

Slocum got a quick kiss as his reward. Then Mina left to return to the top of Carbonate Hill. With some longing, Slocum watched her go. Then he shrugged off the feelings building inside. They wouldn't do him any good. He had to get a box of cartridges. He wasn't going to run short of ammunition this time.

Slocum scooted on his belly until he could peer over the top of the boulder. The Barclay claim looked much as he'd imagined. Two men with rifles stood guard at the base of the hill. At the top prowled Jacobson's gunman who carried the sawed-off shotgun. A fourth claim jumper lounged in the shade near the mouth of the tunnel leading into the hillside.

Slocum decided this one was their leader. He was almost sorry it wasn't Dex Morgan. He could have settled several scores if it had been. Slocum discarded any notion of gunning the men down. He would have to sneak in, as he had told Mina he would.

First a diversion was needed to get the leader's attention focused in the wrong spot.

Like a lizard, Slocum slid back down the boulder. He

had bought a horse and had it tethered half a mile down the arroyo leading to Battle Mountain's steep slopes. He returned to the horse and mounted, riding around the base of the Barclay claim until he came to a small clump of bushes. He gathered dried limbs and dried leaves off scrub oak. When he had a pile, Slocum emptied the gunpowder from a cartridge onto it. A second cartridge provided a small fuse leading off.

Using a lucifer, Slocum lit a dried branch and laid it across the trail of gunpowder. It might take as long as five minutes before the wood burned to the trail and set off the dried debris. When that happened, he wanted to be in position.

Slocum jumped into the saddle and spurred his horse back in the direction he'd come. Before he dismounted again, he heard shouts from the lookout on the far side of the hill. The small blaze had been spotted.

Slocum mounted his rock again and again studied the lay of the land. The men had been pulled from their positions where they might see him. The leader had left the mouth of the mine to investigate the fire. Slocum slipped over the top of the boulder, hit the ground running, and made it to the mouth of the mine without being seen.

"Damned fire's spreading. Who set it? I'm gonna skin you alive if you was cookin' again without tellin' me, Joe," came the leader's angry voice.

Slocum wriggled into the dark mouth of the mine and struggled to get far enough inside to hide before the leader returned. Getting out would be another problem, to be solved when necessary. He swung around and sat with his back against the earthen wall and watched as two claim jumpers came back and stood outlined against the blue sky.

"Well, somebody set it. I smelled gunpowder," the leader said. "Keep a sharp eye out. I'm going to circle around the hill."

Slocum relaxed a mite when the two of them left to patrol the area. They might find his horse. If they did, that would be another problem to solve later on. At the moment, he had to search through the pitch-dark mine for the copy of Barclay's deed.

He began feeling along the walls, growing increasingly apprehensive as he worked in the inky blackness. Barclay hadn't had time to shore up the walls. Slocum had seen too many mines that collapsed and trapped the workers inside. He didn't want to be under a hundred tons of hill if it came crashing down. Barclay had blasted well, but he had been too eager, and had pushed deep into the hill without taking the proper precautions to guarantee safety.

Slocum had to wriggle on his belly after a few yards. The roof had not been secured and he didn't want to even touch it. But he had to. Slow progress took him deeper into the shaft until he wondered how Barclay had managed this much work in such a short time.

His heart almost exploded when he touched something cool and smooth. His first thought had been of snakes. Then he realized that he'd found a stubby candle. Slocum rolled over and looked past his boots to the tiny opening a dozen yards distant. The claim jumpers hadn't returned. He had to take a chance if he wanted to finish in here before he went crazy imagining the roof caving in on him. He pulled a lucifer from his pocket and struck it with his thumbnail. In the brief, blinding flare he saw the candle.

The flame from the wick flicked and danced and gave enough dim light to see by. He continued farther into the mine, dreading every inch. The pale light gave him a sense of distance—and of going forever into the bowels of the earth.

When he came to the end he saw indications of Barclay's pick work. The walls had been scored by a sharp, flat blade. Barclay had begun foundations for support here, almost fifteen yards into the hillside. The combination of rock, dirt, and hard, dried white caliche didn't look promising for gold ore.

Slocum studied the walls and floor more carefully and found a vein with silvery crystal—sylvanite, the telluride of gold.

"I'll be damned. He did hit a rich vein." Slocum shook his head in amazement, wondering if the divining rod had really worked or if Barclay had just been lucky.

Considering all that had happened to the man, Slocum thought it more likely that the divining rod had found the ore.

He had to pull himself away from digging at the ore. Someone would get rich off this claim, and it would be Oscar Jacobson unless he found Barclay's copy of the deed.

The candle sputtered and danced and smoke began to fill the tiny chamber. Slocum moved along on his belly, studying the spots where Barclay had worked on foundations for his support timbers. A hole less than a hand's breadth from another drew Slocum's attention. He held the candle up and was rewarded with a silvery reflection.

He reached into the hold and pulled out a coffee can. The lid had been firmly sealed with candle wax. Slocum peeled it off and popped open the tin. Inside rested the dog-eared deed. From the way it looked, Slocum figured that Barclay must have fingered it and read it and folded and unfolded it a hundred times in the short time it was in his possession.

Slocum slipped the deed into his shirt pocket, wriggled around until he was facing back out the shaft, and started for daylight. He got almost to the mouth before he put out the candle. The intense darkness inside the mine had begun to wear on his nerves. His imagination had run wild with thoughts of the entire hillside coming down around his ears.

He cocked his head to one side and listened hard for stirrings outside. Nothing. No sound, no hint of movement. He wriggled forward, got to his knees, and crawled for daylight.

"What have we got here? Don't think it could be a claim jumper, do you?" Two men stood just outside the mouth of the tunnel.

Slocum threw himself to one side in time to avoid a rifle bullet. The slug buried itself in the dirt and brought down a small shower of debris from the weak roof.

"Come on out, mister, unless you want to die in there."

Slocum had his Colt out by then. When a shape crossed the mouth of the tunnel and was momentarily outlined by the sky, he fired. The claim jumper yelped in pain. Slocum didn't think he had hurt the man bad— not bad enough. A few seconds later the man started cursing a blue streak and Slocum knew he was in a world of trouble.

There was no way out except in front of him. And he had missed his chance to take out one of the four. He faced three men with rifles and shotguns, and one wounded claim jumper, who would prove to be meaner than the other three combined.

Bullets began to sing through the mouth of the mine. Tiny cascades of dirt and rock came down on him. Slocum covered up as best he could and waited. When an incautious head poked up to look in the mine, Slocum fired.

This time there wasn't an answering call of pain. The figure just vanished. Slocum had the gut feeling that there would be only three to worry about now. But he wasn't in any position to celebrate this small victory.

He tried getting to the mouth of the tunnel, thinking he might shoot his way to freedom. A shotgun blast peppered the hill around him, several of the pellets finding their way down the tunnel.

Slocum cursed his bad luck. He had discovered the deed and had no way of getting out of the mine with it. He sucked in a deep breath, got to his knees, and surged forward, Colt blazing.

For a brief instant, he thought his reckless frontal

assault had worked. Then the claim jumpers opened up on him. To leave the mine would have meant bloody death. The fusillade drove him back into the cool interior.

"If you ain't comin' out," shouted the outlaw leader, "then we're gonna have to drag you out."

Slocum reloaded and waited. He knew men like those outside. Patience was not a virtue with them. They would grow nervous, wondering if he had been killed, if he had somehow escaped, a thousand other things. When they came to explore, he would have to be ready. There would not be another chance to get away with his hide in one piece.

It took almost ten minutes before they came for him. Slocum saw one dive across the mouth of the tunnel, trying to draw his fire. He held back, waiting, waiting until his heart almost exploded with the strain.

"We got him, I tell you," an outlaw said.

"He's playin' possum. Be careful."

"I tell you, I nailed him good and proper." The claim jumper showed himself fully at the mine. Slocum could have killed him with one well-placed shot. Still he held back. To kill one would leave a pair—and one of them was wounded. Slocum had learned a long time back that a wounded rat fights harder.

"I see him. He's just sitting at the side. All slumped over. He's dead, I tell you."

"Then get him out of there."

The outlaw got less than a yard into the tunnel when he saw that Slocum hadn't even been wounded. Before he could shout a warning, Slocum slugged him. The blow was clumsy in the tight confines of the shaft, but effective enough. On hands and knees, Slocum crawled past the fallen claim jumper.

"Thought so. Joe always was a stupid son of a bitch."

Standing at the mouth of the mine was the wounded leader. Slocum fired at the same time the man opened up with the shotgun. The last thing Slocum saw was the daylight vanishing in a dust cloud as the roof of the mine gave way because of the loud report from the shotgun.

Tons of dirt and rock crushed down on top of him, trapping him in a coffin of earth.

14

Slocum saw death coming. He got his hands and knees under him and arched his back. The falling tunnel surrounded him, crushed him, pressed him down. He fought to keep his back bent. Only in this way could he hope to survive for even an instant.

The rumbling descent of dirt and rock stopped. Slocum was in complete darkness. Dust clogged his nostrils. When he sneezed, he knew then that he had been successful. Dead men's noses don't itch. He had trapped a small amount of air under his body. But it wouldn't last forever.

Urgency driving him, he began clawing at the loose dirt in front of him. He hoped that the few feet to the tunnel mouth had filled with only loose gravel. If heavy rock had fallen to block his escape, he was as good as dead.

The pressure on his back mounted—or else he weakened. Slocum pawed forward, filling the area under him with dirt as he dug like a terrier after a rat.

Lungs ready to explode, eyes and nose filled with dirt, he thought he'd met his maker when cold wind rushed across his hand. Frantic, he dug faster. The frigid October wind blowing off Battle Mountain gusted into his face. He spat and snorted and got his mouth and nose clear. His eyes popped open. He expected to see the sawed-off shotgun barrel poking into his face.

Only bright blue sky dotted with a few fleecy white clouds greeted him.

Wriggling and kicking, he got free of what might have been his tomb. He brushed the dirt off his new clothing and fumbled out his Colt. Dirt jammed the barrel. If he had fired it, the six-shooter would have blown up in his hand. But there were no targets. The claim jumpers had fled.

Slocum looked at the mineshaft Jonathan Barclay had blasted so well. It had caved in completely. The only evidence of a mine lay under a pile of gravel. He sat on a rock and used a twig to clean out the barrel of his Colt. Slocum wasn't going into Cripple Creek without making sure his sidearm was in good working condition. Jacobson played too many deadly games.

Satisfied with his field stripping and cleaning of the Colt, Slocum started downhill toward the arroyo where he had tethered his newly bought horse. He let out a gusty sigh when he saw the horse was gone. It had been wishing for too much to hope that the claim jumpers wouldn't have found the animal.

His ruse with the fire had drawn them away, but they had carefully checked the surrounding area and found the horse. One good, one bad piece of luck. Slocum touched the pocket where he had stashed the deed. He had to count this as a second piece of good luck.

"And I walked away from a mineshaft cave-in. Not many men do that," he said aloud, adding this final bit of luck to his accounting. Slocum whistled as he made his way around the edge of Barclay's claim and back toward Carbonate Hill. It was harder and slower to walk, but he was alive, and everything would be put right. That belief kept his bootsteps quick-paced and long.

The day was a perfect Rocky Mountain autumn. The air was clean and crisp, and only hints of the coming winter came rushing down to drive away the warmth.

The day turned less than perfect when Slocum got to the bottom of Carbonate Hill. He hadn't thought much on where the claim jumpers had gone after the mine-shaft caved in around his ears. He had shot down two and wounded a third. In the back of his mind he had assumed that the remaining two had left to get patched up.

They had finally figured out what he was hunting for and the two surviving outlaws had gone straight to Mina Barclay's tent to search for the deed. He saw three horses tied to a spindly juniper. One was his stolen mare.

His Colt slipped out of his holster amid a tiny shower of dirt and grit. He cocked it and circled to come up on the claim jumpers from their blind side.

"Where'n hell can it be?" demanded the one Slocum recognized as the leader.

"I'm telling you, there's no reason for that jackass buried alive back there to have been in the mine if it was here," the second said.

"He might have been looking for something else," the leader said. "Damn, but my side hurts. The son of a bitch caught me on a rib. Think he busted it. Hurts every time I suck in a breath."

"If we find the copy of the deed, Morgan's going to give us one hell of a bonus. You'll forget about your pain when you got more gold to spend than you know what to do with."

The pair rummaged through Mina's tent. Slocum didn't know where the woman and Kitty were. It was a good thing they weren't here, or this pair might have tried torturing the information out of them.

Slocum moved on feet as silent as any hunting cat's. He came around the side of the tent, glad that he had taken the precaution of circling. The wounded leader of the pair stood in the door with his sawed-off shotgun pointed downhill. He never saw Slocum as the man moved with lightning speed. Slocum planted his left foot and swung his right around as hard as he could.

The toe of his boot sunk into the claim jumper's belly. The man yowled like a scalded dog and folded up like a jackknife. Slocum spun around, pistol ready.

The uninjured claim jumper had finished ripping the beds apart in his futile search for the duplicate land deed.

"Don't," Slocum said, wishing that the man would anyway. He did. The outlaw's hand flashed for the six-shooter holstered at his side. Slocum's gun barked once. A second shot wasn't needed. He had drilled the outlaw through the head, killing him outright.

He stepped back and covered the outlaw writhing on the ground.

"You busted my ribs. Damn, they hurt!"

"Too bad," Slocum said, his voice cold. He kicked the man in the ribs again to get his attention. "Where's Mrs. Barclay and her daughter?"

"Go to hell!"

He kicked the outlaw again, harder. This time the claim jumper turned white. "Don't do that again. Can't take it. The pain's burning me up inside."

Slocum repeated his question. This time he got an answer.

"Don't know. They wasn't here when we showed up. Honest!"

"You never said an honest word in your life," Slocum said, but he believed the man. "I need some information, and you're just itching to give it to me. Where's Dexter Morgan?"

"He . . . he'll kill me if I say."

Slocum let the man know he was buzzard bait if he didn't talk. He wasn't sure, but he thought he might have busted a couple more ribs convincing the outlaw to talk.

"Outside town," the man gasped, clutching his ribs. "Near Battle Mountain. We got a camp in a little box canyon."

"Is Oscar Jacobson there, too?"

"Jacobson? What'd he want to go there for? We steal the man blind. We rob every gold shipment from the Independence Mine we can."

"Where's the gold go?"

The outlaw's life dimmed. Slocum saw the spark leave the man's eyes as death came closer. Pink froth bubbling on the man's lips told of serious internal injuries. Slocum prodded him again with the toe of his boot. Slocum wasn't going to forget the sight of the shotgun or the sound of the mineshaft falling in on him. No reason to let the man responsible for this and countless other miseries get away with anything.

"Morgan took it after every robbery. Split with a partner. Never knew who. Always told us about the shipments. Always. Damn you, oh God, it hurts so much."

Slocum grabbed the man's collar and dragged him to the top of the dirt trail leading down Carbonate Hill.

"If you make it back, the doc might be able to fix you up. You look like you'd do everyone a favor by crawling straight for Pisgah Graveyard, though. Save having to haul your worthless carcass there when you die."

Slocum took the man's pistol from his holster and flung it downhill. Then he took the three horses, mounted his, and led the other two toward Cripple Creek. The claim jumper gasped and choked behind him, struggling weakly in the dust.

Slocum never looked back. If the man made it, he deserved to live another day. But Slocum didn't think he would get far. He might even die on the spot. It was only fitting. Justice seemed sparse in Cripple Creek— until today.

Slocum rode into Cripple Creek and left the two horses tethered in front of the Golconda. He looked with some longing at the saloon. There was still a mine of gold dust beneath those floors. He might have a chance to go prospecting for some more, but he doubted it. Everything was coming to a head too fast. He dismounted and went inside. Haggerty stood in his familiar place behind the bar. The man's eyebrows shot up so far in surprise that Slocum thought they might just keep on crawling to the back of the man's skull.

"Where's Tiny?" Slocum asked.

"Don't know."

"Betsy?"

"She's upstairs packing. Don't know what's taking her so long."

Slocum went up the stairs, aware of every eye in the saloon following him. He knocked at the door of the first crib. Betsy's querulous voice barked out, "What do you want now, Haggerty? I told you that you ain't gettin' anything for free."

"It's Slocum."

"John? Why didn't you say so? Come on in." The narrow door swung inward. Betsy stood back to let him enter.

"Need to find Tiny," he told her.

"He's over at the Free Coinage Union meeting at the Masonic Hall. It's that brick building down in Old Town." Betsy stared at him and shook her head. "You look a fright. What you been up to?"

"Any notion where I might find Mina?"

Betsy smiled. "Don't go tellin' anybody, but she's down the hall in the last room. She looked like she could use a hot bath, so I snuck her up and let her use the copper tub."

"What about Kitty?"

"She's over at my place out in Poverty Gulch. She's cleaning up the place, the little dickens."

Slocum turned to leave. "Wait, John," Betsy gripped his arm. "What happened?"

"There are four less claim jumpers. Best not to let either Kitty or Mina go back to their tent for a spell. I left some debris there. I'll clean it up later, when I'm done with another chore."

"You sound serious, John. This doesn't have anything to do with Dex Morgan, does it?"

"Rumors surely do fly in a mining town," he said. "I want to see Mina for a few minutes. See we're not disturbed, will you?"

Betsy nodded. Slocum went down the hall to the last room, and entered without knocking. In a high-back copper tub sat Mina Barclay, busily scrubbing her back.

"You need any help?" he asked.

She whirled in the tub, sending soapy water flying. "John! You shouldn't sneak up on me like that."

He reached into his pocket and pulled out the deed. "I found this in a coffee can at the back of the mineshaft. Do you want it?"

"The deed!" Mina cried with excitement. "I surely do."

"Then come and get it." Slocum had business with Dexter Morgan to finish, but he wasn't about to leave without saying a proper goodbye to Mina. He went up against an organized band of road agents and claim jumpers. He might not be coming back.

"I'm all wet," she said, a smile crossing her lips. She pushed back damp brown hair. The sight of her clean tanned skin, the sweep of her fragile neck, the firm breasts just above the bath water all started to make Slocum hard and uncomfortable.

"I don't mind."

She rose from the tub, soap suds running down her sleek body. Her narrow waist emphasized the flare of her hips and the impudent thrust of her breasts. One shapely leg stepped out and tested the floor for purchase. Then came her other. She bent over to pick up a towel. The sight of her damp behind, all taut and inviting like a full moon, took away the last of Slocum's willpower.

He went to her, shedding his clothing as he went.

"And what do I have to do to get the deed?" she asked when he laid it on a dressing table where it wouldn't get wet.

"Just stand where you are and enjoy."

"What?" she teased.

"This." Slocum dropped his denims and moved behind the woman. His hands circled her slender waist and pulled her close. The fleshy moons of her cheeks fit perfectly into the hollow of his body. As Mina bent forward to rest her hands on the side of the copper tub, the perfection of the fit became even more obvious to both of them.

He reached around and cupped both her dangling breasts in his hands. When he squeezed down, catching the nipples between his thumbs and forefingers, Mina groaned with pleasure. She began moving her hips in a slow. grinding circle. Slocum's crotch burned with desire now.

He almost exploded when she reached back between her legs and found the dangling pouch filled with his balls. She kneaded them the same way he worked over her breasts, slowly, gently, with increasing urgency.

"Move," she said. "I love the feel of you inside me, but move! You're driving me wild!"

"Good."

His hand left the woman's firm breasts and stroked over her belly, along her sides, up and across her shoulders. Slocum pulled back slightly, his iron-hard shaft sliding from the slick sheath of female flesh. Inside was warm and wet. Out was cool and dry. He preferred to be buried all the way up the woman.

He shoved his hips forward as Mina bent further forward. She gave his balls another squeeze that caused Slocum to gasp. He fought to keep from coming. He wanted this to last forever.

"Move, John, I need it, I need *you!*"

He slid forward again, going deeper into her yearning body. As he stroked back and forth, Mina began rotating her hips in a slow, passionate circle. The combined motions set fires ablaze within Slocum that refused to die down. He stroked faster and faster until he found the rhythm that gave them both all the pleasure they could stand.

Mina gasped and sagged forward, her knees turning

to butter. Slocum caught her around the waist and picked her up, making sure that her clinging body never left his.

He swung her around. She gasped and stiffened with desire again. This time Slocum was unable to hold back. He shuddered and spilled his seed deep within her.

Together they sank to the floor. Mina turned around to face him. Her eyes blazed and the smile on her face was lewd. "More?" she asked hopefully.

"Can't," Slocum said. "Maybe I shouldn't have taken the time for this, but you were so damned appealing, I couldn't resist."

"I'm glad. Don't start resisting. Neither of us would like that." She kissed him and fires that had died down were rekindled.

Ater they had finished making love a second time, Slocum knew he had to go. Dex Morgan might have heard about his four men being killed by now. If he laid a trap, if Slocum lost the element of surprise, if any of a dozen things went wrong, Slocum would be as dead as if he had been killed in the mineshaft collapse.

"What happened at the mine, John?" Mina Barclay asked. She dried her hands on a towel and ran her fingers over the dirty scrap of paper. "You've got that look."

"Don't go on back to your tent for a while. Spend some time with Betsy. I know Poverty Gulch isn't much, but you'll be safer there for the time being."

"For how long?"

"Not long," he answered, buckling his gunbelt securely. He checked to be sure his Colt slid easily into his hand. He took a damp towel and wiped off the inside of the holster and tried again. This time the weapon leaped to his grip as if it had come alive.

"You're going after them alone. That's a damned stupid thing to do. Why," Mina said, sputtering as she tried to think of how stupid it was, "that's something I'd expect from Jonathan!"

"There's a judge coming to town this weekend. Show him the deed. Maybe Jacobson hasn't bought him. But avoid the Denver lawyer. He's thrown in with Jacobson. I'm sure of that."

"Where are you going, John? Wait for Tiny. Get him or some others to go with you."

"This is between me and Morgan. Jacobson can be taken care of later. I don't want Morgan turning tail and running." He checked the load in his Colt and spun the cylinder. "I want him for myself."

"Why is this something personal? What's he done to you?"

Slocum almost didn't tell her. Then he decided there could be no harm. "Morgan is the road agent who held us up on the way into Cripple Creek."

"And?" she prodded. "There's more. What is it?"

"He killed your husband and set fire to the town."

Mina Barclay turned white and leaned back against the dresser for support. She said nothing more as Slocum left to find Dexter Morgan.

15

Slocum considered stopping by the Masonic Hall and getting Tiny to ride along with him. He decided against this. Involving the giant miner in something that wasn't his concern didn't set well with Slocum. He might be going up against Morgan and a dozen others alone, but he had the advantage of surprise. If he went riding into this box canyon hideout with Tiny and others with him, that advantage might evaporate.

He snorted and shook his head. He was kidding himself. He knew why he rode alone. It was the way it had always been—the way he worked best. He wanted the pleasure of taking Morgan out knowing it was he who pulled the trigger.

Memory of the mineshaft collapsing on him firmed his resolve. Morgan hadn't been there ordering his death, but those had been his men. The claim jumpers had done worse than Slocum intended to do to them, and Morgan was chief among them.

He'd take care of Oscar Jacobson later. First he had to step on some human rattlers.

He took the road to the Independence Mine and hunted for a likely formation in the hills surrounding Battle Mountain. From what the claim jumper he had

167

interrogated said, the box canyon lay off a small path, hardly one worth noticing. Slocum found plenty of those, but only one with fresh horse droppings to show that someone had ridden the trail within the past twenty-four hours.

His cold green eyes studied the hills. This had to be the place. If he'd been looking for a hideout, he could not have chosen a better spot. The high canyon walls gave sentries dozens of places to watch unobserved. A rider would be spotted fifteen minutes before getting to the canyon mouth.

Slocum reined his mare around and kept going, looking for a path to the top of the steep, jagged canyon walls. He found a rubble-strewn path within the hour and started the protesting horse up it. Before he had gone halfway, he had to dismount. The strain of stepping across treacherous gravel carrying a rider proved too much for the animal.

An hour of climbing brought him to the summit. He smiled. A recent campfire showed that Morgan's sentries sometimes patrolled here. That meant an easier path down into their camp.

Every sense straining, Slocum cautiously explored. He smelled the posted sentry before he saw or heard the man. The pungent odor of tobacco rose from over the crest of the hill. From under a lip of rock, a man could scan the road into the canyon without being seen.

Slocum thanked his lucky stars. If he had ridden into the mouth of the canyon, he would have been spotted. As it was, he might have been noticed and discounted as a passing traveler. He tethered his horse and checked his Colt. He took a buck knife from his gear and slipped it into the gunbelt at the small of his back.

Sniffing the air, he homed in on the sentry. The tobacco smoke turned blue in the clear mountain air and rose in a plume, untouched by the erratic mountain winds. Slocum picked his way down a rocky path until he saw a red checked shirt and a stained brown Stetson.

A bit further down the path let him see the man wearing them.

The sentry paid no attention to his back. His eyes scanned the approach to the canyon. Slocum waited a few minutes to figure out how the man would signal camp if he saw intruders. When the sentry reached over and fingered a mirror, Slocum was satisfied. He moved as silently as the rising smoke.

A gunshot would echo down the canyon and alert everyone in the camp. Slocum used his knife. One hand circled the man's face and caught a handful of greasy beard. Slocum tightened on this convenient grip and yanked the man's head back, cutting off any scream. His right hand drove the point of his knife into the man's back. The sentry jerked around for a few seconds, then sank down.

Slocum followed him to the ground. He studied the sheer canyon walls for any indication that another sentry had seen the death. Nothing. Slocum peered over the rocky verge and down to the floor of the box canyon. The canyon made a sharp-angled turn. From the box a dozen cooking fires sent smoke aloft. The sound of horses echoed along the rocky walls and Slocum saw riders moving around in the safety of their hideout. He made out the spot where the sentry was most likely to flash a mirror signal. From that point Dex Morgan could get all his men onto horses and in fighting trim long before even a fast-moving column of cavalry could trap them.

Satisfied that the camp still believed itself inviolate, Slocum went back up the path to the top of the ridge. He hiked along it until he found the path leading to the camp below. He could ride; the narrow path looked safe enough. But if he did he might warn Morgan. The sentry had no animal. Slocum pulled his Winchester from the saddle sheath, made certain he had all the ammunition he could carry, and then started walking down the path.

It took twenty minutes to get to the canyon floor. Along the way Slocum had plenty of opportunity to study the layout of the camp. All the defense focused on the mouth of the canyon. No one expected attack from above or from behind.

Slocum had taken out four of the claim jumpers at Jonathan Barclay's mine. That left at least six—ten had attacked Mina at the mine.

Slocum didn't want to bother with five.

He wanted Dexter Morgan.

As he came off the trail to the corral at the back of the box canyon, he had counted four in camp. The sentry he had killed made five. If they had one more guard posted, this accounted for all the outlaws.

One road agent came out of a low-roofed bunkhouse. He looked up in surprise when he saw Slocum. His mouth worked like a steelhead trout's when pulled out of water. Slocum swung up his rifle and fired. The bullet caught the man high in the shoulder and spun him around. A second shot finished him.

He had three to go, and the element of surprise had gone.

"What's all that infernal ruckus out there?" another outlaw shouted from inside the bunkhouse. "You're not spooking the horses again, are you, Luke?"

The man stood for an instant in the bunkhouse door. Luke lay face down in the dirt. Slocum got off a shot but the man had ducked back into the bunkhouse. A real gunfight looked to be forming.

Slocum didn't hurry. He walked briskly around the corral and got away from the bunkhouse door. No need to make it easier for the outlaw inside to shoot out. Without windows, the only entry point looked to be the door, but Slocum had to be sure.

The thatched roof might provide a way for the trapped outlaw to get free. Slocum decided to cut off this path of escape. He reached into his pocket and pulled out a lucifer.

"Burn," he said as he tossed the blazing lucifer onto

the roof. It took several seconds for the fire to get a foothold. Then it blazed merrily.

The road agent came out with his six-shooter firing. Lead sprayed wildly. Slocum waited for the man to turn before he squeezed off a round. The bullet caught the man squarely in the gut. The impact knocked him back into the side of the bunkhouse. The outlaw staggered away from the burning building. Slocum followed, rifle ready for another shot. The outlaw collapsed over a corral rail.

Slocum kicked the gun from the man's hand. "Where's Morgan?" he asked.

"You shot me," the man moaned. "I . . . I'm all liquid inside. Nothing feels right."

"Where's Dexter Morgan?" Slocum repeated. The outlaw slumped. The wind coming up the canyon caused the man's arms to sway back and forth. Slocum didn't bother checking to see if the man was dead. He was.

Slocum watched the fire grow more intense. Fifty-foot-high tongues of flame shot into the air. Slocum turned the horses loose from the corral and let them race to freedom down the canyon. He found a low rise and settled on it, his rifle across his knees. Morgan and another rider were down the canyon. At least, he hoped one of them was Dex Morgan.

He took out a twisted-up quirly and scowled. It was better than nothing, he decided, although he'd have preferred a fine cigar. Perhaps a Havana. He had enough gold dust in his poke to afford one now. Slocum lit up and puffed away. He just finished grinding out the butt under his heel when two clouds of dust rose in the distance.

Dex Morgan had come to find out what had happened in his camp.

The two riders approached slowly. Slocum sat rock-still, in no hurry. He had done this before, during the War. Patience was a virtue for a sniper. Never rush. Always take the good shots. Slocum sighted and got one man lined up properly. The distance was still too great for the Winchester. He wished he had a .69 Sharps with a tripod.

The riders came closer. He heard muffled curses. ". . . I'll skin that lousy son of a bitch alive!" exclaimed Dex Morgan.

"Don't be so hard on Luke. He don't know better," said the other. The distance was still too great for Slocum to decide which was Morgan.

"If he's been screwing around again and burned down the bunkhouse, I *will* cut his ears off and nail them to the door."

One man made an angry gesture. Slocum decided this was Morgan. He lined up the shiny bead in the iron vee sights, then frowned. The bead was too bright. The shiny spot blocked the target. He spit on his finger and dipped it in the dirt. A quick swipe across the front sight took care of the shining sighting bead.

Slocum lined up, decided on windage, corrected, and fired. The man on the right jerked back and fell off his horse. He had made a clean shot at damned near two hundred yards.

"Slocum!" bellowed the remaining rider.

Slocum cursed under his breath. He had shot the wrong rider. The one he'd taken for Morgan had been the henchman arguing for his wayward friend, Luke.

Slocum levered in another round, but the moment had passed. Morgan was too wily to stay in the saddle in an exposed position. He had spurred for a tumble of rock a hundred yards to his left. Hunched over his horse's neck as he was, Slocum had no good shot on the rider.

He fired, hitting the horse high in the shoulder. The animal stumbled and sent Dex Morgan head over heels into the dust. Slocum hated the notion of killing an innocent horse, but to get Morgan he'd kill every horse in every remuda in Colorado.

"You won't get me that easy, Slocum," the outlaw called. "I remember you from the days with Quantrill.

You were a lily-livered bastard even then. Always turning tail and running. Never fighting like the rest of us."

Slocum silently reloaded. He knew Morgan only sought to anger him. Slocum wasn't even certain that Morgan knew where the deadly shots had come from. There were half a dozen good spots for a sniper at this end of the box canyon.

He began walking behind the hill he had chosen for his post. Slocum sought to circle behind Morgan and trap him in the canyon. It would be only a matter of time before a good shot presented itself. He hadn't ridden with Morgan for years, but he remembered that the scar-faced man had no patience. Always edgy, always moving, he shot first and considered his actions later.

Dex Morgan had been like most of Quantrill's Raiders. That was another reason Slocum had never quite fit in.

"Where are you, Slocum? You running away again? You turning into a stinking coward, like you did after the Lawrence raid?"

Slocum stood behind a low rise. If he had estimated properly, Morgan hid on the far side of the hill. He trudged up the back slope and cautiously peered over the top of the rise. Not ten yards below him, partially hidden by a tumble of rocks, hid Dexter Morgan. Slocum pulled the Winchester up and into position. He rested it on a rock for steadiness, got his sight picture, and squeezed the trigger.

The recoil jolted his shoulder. Dex Morgan stiffening and falling forward was his reward for the small discomfort.

Slocum started to check the result of his marksmanship, then stopped. Patience. That was the thing outlaws like Morgan lacked. It might not be the only difference between them, but Slocum wanted to keep this one trait distinct. Morgan would have rushed downhill to check had the tables been turned.

If he had missed, Slocum would have been waiting with a pistol and ready to kill.

Slocum went over the shot again in his head. Everything looked good. The memory of the sights, of Morgan in the right spot, of the way he jerked when the bullet hit, all that seemed as it should. Something else struck Slocum as wrong.

He decided he had nothing to lose but a few minutes if he sat and waited. Slocum kept the Winchester pointed in the general direction of the outlaw. He wasn't sure where Dex Morgan's body had rolled. That was what bothered him most.

Five minutes passed. Slocum settled into a more comfortable position by the time ten had come around. Then he saw a flash of sunlight on a gun barrel. Morgan had been playing possum.

"Where are you, Slocum?" came the outlaw's angry cry. "You son of a bitch! Come down and fight like a man. Don't go settin' up there takin' potshots at me!"

Morgan tried to run from the base of the hill toward the corral area. The instant he poked his head up, Slocum fired. Morgan's hat went flying into the air. But the claim jumper got off a series of shots that forced Slocum to duck for cover. When he looked around the side of the rock he used as a shield, Morgan had reached the corral.

Slocum got off another shot, but missed.

"Why are you doing this, Slocum? Why hunt me down like an animal?"

"You *are* an animal," Slocum snapped back. "Didn't want to shoot your damned horse. I was aiming at you. You've been a pain in the ass for too long."

"I'm sorry I didn't kill you when I had the chance during the stagecoach robbery."

"You weren't sure if you recognized me or not. It's been a lot of years, Morgan, and we didn't ride together that long."

"We can work this out, Slocum. This is profitable territory. Gold everywhere. We can get rich."

"Not when you have to hand over most of what you

steal to Oscar Jacobson. Silent partners tend to want more and more for their information."

"You stinking son of a bitch!" Morgan cut loose with a wild barrage of shots. None came close. Slocum slipped back down the hill and retraced his footsteps until he came out with a good view of the corral. Morgan hunted desperately for a horse; Slocum had already turned them loose. The fire and the gunshots had made sure that the animals were long gone down the canyon. They might not stop running until they got to Cripple Creek.

Slocum got off another shot at Morgan. Then the Winchester jammed. He tried to clear it, but the spent brass had caught inside the receiver. Slocum put down the rifle. His Colt was as good a weapon as was made. It would serve him well now.

"Why'd you have to go and burn down the bunk-house?" Morgan called.

Slocum knew the man played for time. Why?

"I was hoping you were inside," Slocum answered. He kept moving, trying to keep Morgan boxed up in the back of the canyon. He couldn't let the outlaw escape. Not now. He had a real score to settle with the man. Dex Morgan had killed Jonathan Barclay and set fire to Cripple Creek. He was in cahoots with Jacobson. He robbed stages—and took forty dollars in greenbacks that rightly belonged to Slocum.

Slocum wanted him. He moved around until he got a clear view of the area beyond the corral. He had thought Morgan might try to reach the trail leading to the canyon walls.

"Goodbye, Slocum," came the outlaw's cold voice.

Slocum spun, Colt coming up and already firing.

The roar of a shotgun deafened Slocum, but the buckshot missed him. His bullet had flown straight and true. If Morgan hadn't warned him, he would be lying dead in the dust.

His shot had caught Morgan in the heart. The impact

had caused the shotgun to rise. The shot had gone in the air, over Slocum's head. Slocum didn't have to check his handiwork this time. He knew Morgan was dead. How the man had gotten around behind him he didn't know.

It no longer mattered. He stood staring at the outlaw's body. Morgan had a large bandage on his left arm from the previous fight with Slocum. This time the bullet's point of entry had been right on target.

Slocum looked around for a horse. They had all fled. He waited for the fire to burn itself out in the bunkhouse, then searched through the ashes for gold or scrip. He found a few charred greenbacks. He thrust them into his pocket. He might find a banker willing to swap them for whole notes. He doubted it but he didn't want to leave the canyon empty-handed.

Slocum took one last look at Dex Morgan. The outlaw lay on his back, huge blue flies already drawn to an easy meal. The buzzards would soon circle down.

It seemed too easy an end for Morgan.

Slocum started the hike up the trail to the top of the canyon where he had left his horse. It was a ways back to Cripple Creek, and he still had business there—with Oscar Jacobson.

16

John Slocum was bone-tired by the time he got back to Cripple Creek. It had taken him only twenty minutes to go from the top of the rocky walls to the floor of the box canyon. Hiking steadily and refusing to give in to fatigue, he had gotten back to his horse in a little over an hour. The climb had been wearing on him, and the ride to town was even worse.

The only thing keeping him from total exhaustion was the knowledge that Dexter Morgan wouldn't make any more women into widows, that he wouldn't rob any more stage coaches, and that he would not set another devastating fire.

Morgan was dead. Oscar Jacobson remained.

Riding into Cripple Creek, Slocum saw no one in the streets. He wondered if it had become a ghost town. Faint howls and shouts and cries came from the Masonic Hall. He decided that the miners had themselves a rally going and that this had taken the people off the streets.

He dismounted and went into the Golconda Saloon. Only Haggerty was inside. Slocum had never seen the man look so frightened.

"Slocum, I'm glad you're here. They're over at the

Hall. They're gonna burn the place down. I swear it!"

"Whiskey," Slocum said, dropping a coin on the bar. He knocked back the shot and motioned to Haggerty for another. "You're talking about the union miners?"

"Jacobson won't give them their raise. They're threatening to finish the job the fire started. And they mean to burn down the saloon."

"So clear out."

"Slocum, he'd fire me if I left!"

"Can't help you, Haggerty. Jacobson let me go. I don't work here and even if I did, I wouldn't get myself killed just to protect you—or the Golconda."

"You're telling me to hightail it out of here?"

"I'm not telling you anything, except that another round would be mighty nice."

Haggerty paced like a caged animal. The sound of miners gathering in the street convinced him to run. "You're making a mistake, Slocum," Haggerty said. "Jacobson would give you a big reward for protecting the Golconda."

"Bet he'd give it to you, too," Slocum said. "All you'd have to do is face down a hundred angry miners."

That was enough to set Haggerty running for the back room. Slocum heard the back door slam. He reached over the bar and got himself the entire bottle. It felt good going down, but Slocum wasn't looking to get drunk.

He still had a knotty problem to solve—and that problem was Oscar Jacobson.

Slocum worked on the bottle while he worked on how best to solve the dilemma presented by Jacobson. It came slowly. Without the fake deeds, Mina Barclay's copy of the claim had to stand, no matter how the lawyer, Grassley, or Jacobson testified. The removal of the fraudulent claims made it easier for the other miners to get back their claims, too. The law wouldn't back Jacobson in the face of a dozen or more irate miners, each supporting the others' claims.

Slocum finished off the whiskey in his glass and

walked out of the Golconda. He cast a long look at the floor. A passel of gold dust remained for an enterprising man. He wondered if he would get the chance to continue his "mining." Somehow, he doubted it. After today, Cripple Creek would likely get too hot for him.

He rode to the bank and then went around the block, carefully studying the way the doors and windows were placed. He had robbed enough banks in his day to know what to look for. The safe inside would take more than a few sticks of dynamite to open. He didn't even consider blowing it. He had to get at the fake deeds while the clerk had them out.

To do that he needed a diversion.

Across the street from the bank stood a half-built store. The construction crew working on it had been diverted to repair buildings in the part of Cripple Creek partially burned to the ground. Slocum looked over the store and began gathering debris and stacking it so that flames would show through the unframed windows and doors. If luck rode with him, the building itself wouldn't be much the worse after the fire burned itself out.

He dropped a lucifer into the pile and walked quickly across the street. He peered in the window and smiled. The land office clerk had his precious boxes of fake deeds spread out around him. To one side stood a man with arms crossed. Slocum recognized him as one of the gunmen who had ridden as bodyguard for Jacobson.

He went to the door and shouted, "Fire! There's a fire across the street! Everybody out! It's spreading fast!"

He stepped back and let the few bank patrons rush out. The tellers were more orderly in closing down their windows and locking their drawers before running like the devil chased them. But the clerk and his guard stood their ground. The clerk began scooping up the papers and trying to stuff them into a file box.

Slocum slipped in, his Colt out.

"Don't bother," he told the clerk. His gun shifted to

cover the guard, who reached for his own six-shooter. Slocum motioned for the guard to drop his gun.

"Jacobson is gonna eat you alive for this, Slocum," the guard said in a low, gravelly voice. Slocum saw scars crisscrossing the man's throat and wondered if this was as loud as he could speak.

"Go tell him all about it." The guard sidled out, then took off at a dead run.

"Don't kill me," the clerk whined. "They made me do it. Jacobson and Grassley. They made me! I know all about the claim jumping. And Jacobson's using the union to force out his partners in the Independence Mine, too."

"Burn the fake deeds," Slocum ordered.

"What?" The idea of destroying papers, even fake documents, tore at the being of this bureaucrat. The motion of Slocum's Colt convinced him to obey.

Slocum had to give the man a lucifer to light the papers. When the clerk finally got the fire going, he stood pale-faced and shaking. "Mr. Jacobson's not going to like this. You shouldn't have let Whispers go like that."

"Is this all the fake deeds?" Slocum asked.

"That's the lot," the clerk said. From the way he spoke, Slocum thought he was telling the truth. The clerk was too frightened to do anything else. "Can I go? The fire. . . ."

Slocum glanced across the street. The fire had burned itself out and had left the shell of the store unscathed. He holstered his Colt and backed out.

The clerk saw that the fire danger had passed, but he knew another menace loomed. He grabbed his coat and got to the door before he saw Whispers coming back, with Oscar Jacobson a half step behind. Both men carried rifles.

"Hold it, Slocum," Jacobson bellowed. "Whispers, take him out."

Slocum drew smoothly but the rifle had the greater range. He dived and rolled under the boardwalk. Bullets

dug into the wood above his head, then moved closer as
Whispers got the range.

As suddenly as the fusillade started, it stopped. Replacing the rifle reports came angry shouts.

"There they are. Let's talk, Jacobson."

Slocum rolled from under the boardwalk. Whispers's
arms were held by two burly miners. They dragged him
off. Frank Dennis jerked the rifle from Jacobson's
hands.

"What do you men want? This is hardly the time or
place . . ."

"It's both. We want our raise," Dennis demanded.
"We're striking the Independence Mine unless you
agree. And it's gonna be hard on everyone, especially if
you try to bring in non-union workers."

"Three dollars a shift? That seems fair," Jacobson
said. He glanced over his shoulder at Slocum. "Let's
draw up an agreement."

For several seconds Frank Dennis and the other
miners just stood and stared. Someone said, "He gave in
awful damned easy. Why? He's been stonewalling us up
till now."

"I'll tell you why," Slocum said. "Jacobson is using
you to drive out the other owners of the mine. He figured you would make life hell and show how unprofit-
able the Independence might be. He could buy them for
next to nothing."

"As long as we get our pay hike, what's the difference what these robber barons do to each other?" This
seemed to be a sentiment shared by the miners.

"He had Jonathan Barclay killed. He wanted *all* the
gold in the District. He's one hell of a greedy bastard."
Slocum quickly spoke of the claim jumping. He wished
the land office clerk had been there, but the man had
taken off like a frightened jackrabbit.

"We heard tell of this. You got proof?" Frank Dennis
held Jacobson by the collar, keeping the man from following the clerk.

"I do. I'll swear in court to it, also." Mina Barclay

pushed through the crowd. "Mr. Slocum is correct in everything he says. I have my husband's deed right here. Jacobson sent men to take possession of the claim illegally.

"There's nothing to prove that," said Jacobson. "There aren't any fake deeds to be found." Jacobson glanced over to Whispers, who nodded. "Without such proof of fraud . . ." Jacobson smiled.

Slocum cursed his stupidity. He had destroyed the evidence needed to show that Jacobson was trying to do some claim jumping by doctoring county records. Mina could get clear title to her husband's mine and the other independent miners would keep their property, but Jacobson would walk away scot free.

Most of the men who might have testified against him were dead. Slocum didn't want to bet that Whispers would count for much, and the clerk would say whatever Jacobson told him.

"I'll press charges against him," Mina Barclay said. "The judge is due in town this weekend."

"Yeah, me and Betsy's gettin' hitched!" Tiny called out.

"I'll take this all the way to the Denver District Court if necessary," she said.

"He really been jerking us around?" a miner asked. Others who had had their claims jumped began talking with those from the big Battle Mountain mine.

Slocum heard the tenor of the crowd's words begin to change. "This son of a bitch is the one who caused us all our trouble. And he burned down the town to destroy the land office."

This spread faster than the fire. Jacobson shouted denials, but the miners grabbed him and carried him along.

"John, what are they doing? Taking him to the jail?" Mina asked.

"Reckon they're going to string him up. They looked mighty angry at him for burning down the town."

"But I said I'd prefer charges. They can't hang him.

He hasn't had a fair trial."

"You have any doubts about him being guilty?"

"No, but . . ." Mina gasped when she saw the knotted rope arc up and go over a sign. Jacobson was shoved up into the saddle of a nervous horse. Barely had the rope been dropped over Jacobson's neck when the horse bolted. The snap of the man's neck echoed down the street.

"Oh, dear God," Mina said, turning away.

The crowd still wasn't satisfied. Tiny's voice drowned out the others with his bull-throated bellow, "What about the lawyer? Bring out the Denver lawyer. He's as guilty as Jacobson!"

Within five minutes a second body swung slowly in the cold wind blowing down Cripple Creek's main street.

Tiny came over to Slocum and Mina and said, "Hanging was too good for the lawyer. But that takes care of Cripple Creek's big problems. All we got to do now is rebuild—and I got to get hitched to Betsy!"

"Looks like the worst is over," Slocum said. Mina stared up at him with the eyes of a stranger. She took a step away. "What's wrong?" he asked.

"You let them murder Jacobson and Grassley. You didn't even try to stop them."

He started to tell her how he had killed Dex Morgan and the others, then paused.

"Why does that bother you? You said they were guilty. Jacobson killed your husband, or ordered it done. Grassley tried to cheat you out of your gold mine. Isn't this what they deserved?"

"They didn't get a fair trial."

"They were guilty. The sheriff's not arrived in town yet and the judge comes up from Colorado Springs once every two or three months. Justice comes quick in a boom town like this."

"It's not supposed to be this way. There are laws."

"Jacobson would have ended up at the end of a rope, anyway. Burning good, decent people out of their houses and businesses isn't a good way to win friends."

"If the jury had found him guilty and that was the sentence, that'd have been all right," she said primly "But this? He was murdered."

"If this was Kansas City, you might be right. This is Cripple Creek. What happened wasn't according to the law, but it was justice being served." He saw that the argument wasn't convincing her. "Let's get out of the street and—"

"John," she said. The sharpness in his voice told him that she had come to a decision that wasn't going to set well with him. "I'm taking Kitty and we're going back to Kansas City."

"I thought you and me—"

"John, please," she said, cutting him off "This is no fit place to raise a child." She heaved a deep sigh. "Or for me to live. Jonathan kept us on the fringes of civilization for too long. I *like* Kansas City. I only came out here to be with my husband."

"You're a rich woman. Your husband's claim may not be as rich as the Independence Mine, but it'll leave you well off."

"You can have it. I don't care. I just want to be done with this awful place." She looked back over her shoulder at the two hanged criminals. "I lost Jonathan here. I don't want to lose my own life—or Kitty's."

"I don't want your claim," Slocum said.

"Here, take it. It's yours. Keep it. Give it away. Do what you want with it." She stared up into his eyes, her face forlorn. "I'm sorry, John. Really. I wanted it to be different."

"I can go with you," he said. As the words came out he knew it wouldn't work. Mina Barclay wanted a world completely different from the one he lived in. He would feel like a bird in a cage in polite Kansas City society. Even with Mina, he would not like it. In time he would come to hate her for forcing him to make such a decision.

She shook her head. She knew the answer, too.

"I'll see to the claim," Slocum said. "A man owes me a big favor." He thought of the man he had saved in the fire. The man and his entire family had come to Cripple Creek looking for wealth. This would give them a touch of it. If they kept half the gold from the Barclay claim and sent the other half to Mina, she would be well off.

"Oh, John," she said. She clung to him and then pushed away. Their eyes met and Mina tried to smile. Then the woman turned and hurried off.

Slocum might have gone after her. He might have stopped her. But it would have been a mistake. They lived in different worlds.

He went to his horse and mounted. Patting the poke of gold dust in his pocket, he decided he had enough to get him a bit farther west. Where, he didn't care. Tiny and Betsy might be angry that he'd missed their wedding, but they would get over it.

Slocum wasn't sure he could face Mina again, knowing that the roads they traveled had reached a fork.

John Slocum rode out of Cripple Creek, turned up his collar to the cold wind blowing off the Rockies, and never looked back.